# Gag Me With a Spoon

*Crime Fiction Inspired by Music of the 1980s*

*Edited by J. Alan Hartman*

White City

Press

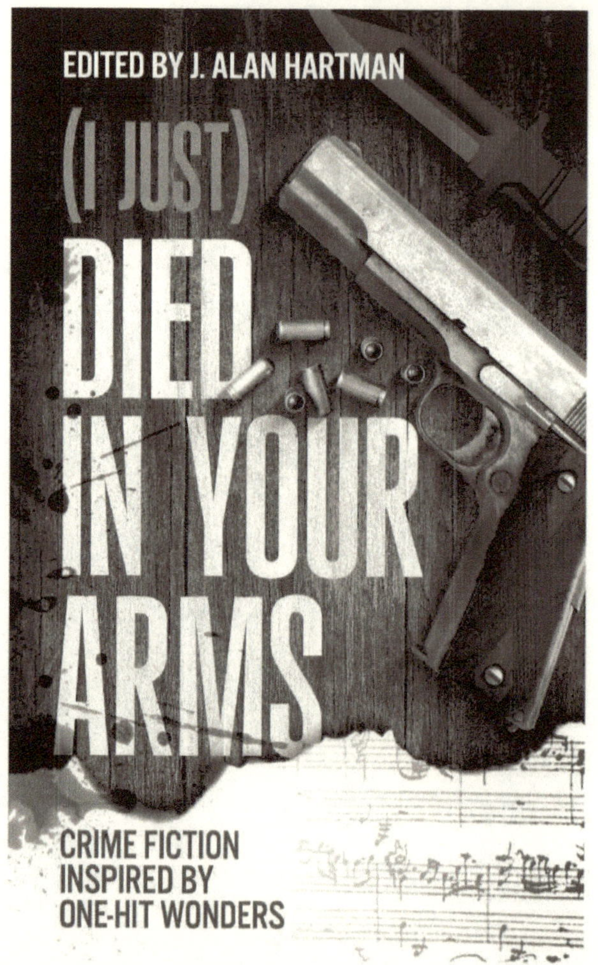


*Hitting the charts only once isn't just unfortunate...it's a crime.*
Over the decades, tons of musical artists and groups have had a hit song that has lived on long after the tune topped the charts and is often looked upon fondly for decades to come. For some musicians, this may be the only the song they're ever known for and they fade into obscurity soon thereafter. These are affectionately known as "one-hit wonders," and are much celebrated by fans and music publications, particularly on September 25th each year on One-Hit Wonder Day

12 of today's best short story authors have taken their favorite one-hit wonders and reimagined them as the influence for some pretty heinous crimes. *(I Just) Died in Your Arms* features a decades-spanning collection of immediately recognizable hit songs turned into stories from the amazing talents of Vinnie Hansen, Jeanne DuBois, Josh Pachter, J.M. Taylor, Christine Verstraete, Sandra Murphy, Joseph S. Walker, Wendy Harrison, Bev Vincent, Leone Ciporin, Adam Gorgoni and Barb Goffman.

**Paperback ISBN: 9781963479027  eBook ISBN 9781963479010**

With a career spanning over 50 years, Aerosmith has been a trend-setter in the world of rock and roll. From early hits such as "Dream On" and "Sweet Emotion" to their legendary collaboration with Run DMC for a cover of "Walk This Way" to their contribution of "Don't Wanna Miss a Thing" on the soundtrack for *Armageddon*, Aerosmith has proved time and again to be a band capable of reinvention and constant influence on the music scene.

With their 2024 announcement that the band will no longer tour, 16 crime fiction authors have come together to produce an anthology paying tribute to some of Aerosmith's greatest hits and their studio albums. This literary trip across the rock and roll landscape is courtesy of multi-award winning editor Michael Bracken with stories by Ed Ridgley, Bill Baber, Eve Fisher. Avram Lavinsky, John C. Breuning, Jeffrey Marks, Mary Dutta, Tom Mead, Steve Liskow, Joseph S. Walker, Adam Meyer, John M. Floyd, Leone Ciporin, M.E. Proctor, Tom Milani and Jim Winter.

**Paperback ISBN: 9781963479539 — eBook ISBN: 9781963479522**

Manilow also created a legendary musical crime in his song *Copacabana*, telling the story of feather-wearing dancer Lola who is caught between bartender Tony and patron Rico as the two men vie for her affections…and ultimately meet untimely ends.

Now, 13 crime author fans of Barry (affectionately known as "Fanilows") take on other songs from his collection of hits to tell all new stories of love, life, relationships and other situations gone horribly wrong. All the hits are here, as well as a few lesser-known tracks.

As Manilow sings, "there was blood and a single gunshot. But just who shot who?"

This collection features all new stories from Karen Keeley, Linda Kay Hardie, Adam Gorgoni, Maya St. Clair, Matt McGee, Laurie Stevens, Caleb Weinhardt, Kurtis Rupé, Recita Clemons, J. M. Taylor, John M. Floyd, T. Fox Dunham, Christine Verstraete and Shari Held.


Paperback ISBN: 9781963479706
eBook ISBN: 9781963479690

# Gag Me With a Spoon

*Crime Fiction Inspired by Music of the 1980s*

*Edited by J. Alan Hartman*

This edition published by White City Press

An imprint of Misti Media LLC

https://whitecitypress.com

Available in both Paperback and eBook Editions

1 2 3 4 5 6 7 8 9 10

Copyright Respective Authors © 2025

Paperback ISBN: 9781963479980

eBook ISBN: 9781963479997

# Acknowledgements

*Sappho's Girl* by Linda Kay Hardie
Inspired by *Jesse's Girl* (Rick Springfield 1980)

*Motivation* by Steve Shrott
Inspired by *9 to 5* (Dolly Parton 1980)

*In the Air Tonight* by Marilyn Todd
Inspired by *In the Air Tonight* (Phil Collins 1981)

*Our Lips Are Sealed* by Teresa Inge
Inspired by *Our Lips Are Sealed* (The Go-Gos 1981)

*The Safety Dance* by Michael Bracken
Inspired by *The Safety Dance* (Men Without Hats 1982)

*Uptown Girl* by John M. Floyd
Inspired by *Uptown Girl* (Billy Joel 1983)

*Girls Just Wanna Have Fun* by Lesley A. Diehl
Inspired by *Girls Just Wanna Have Fun* (Cyndi Lauper 1983)

*Marge and Dot Go Rogue* by Sandra Murphy
Inspired by *The Heat Is On* (Glenn Frey 1984)

*That Damn Car* by Shari Held
Inspired by *Danger Zone* (Kenny Loggins 1986)

*The Future's So Bright, I Gotta Wear Shades* by Joseph S. Walker
Inspired by *The Future's So Bright, I Gotta Wear Shades* (Timbuk 3 1986)

*Free Fallin'* by Josh Pachter
Inspired by *Free Fallin'* (Tom Petty and the Heartbreakers 1989)

# Contents

## *An Epically Rad and Wicked Anthology*

As a card-carrying member of Generation-X, I will live and die on the hill that the music of my generation is infinitely better than that of any other. Sure, every age group says this of their music, but it's pretty hard to prove compared to the songs of the 1980s.

The Decade of Decadence contributed more one-hit wonders and songs that would survive into the future than any other decade that came before it. Even now, in the first quarter of the 21st century, it's fairly difficult for a song from the 1980s to play on the radio or a Spotify list without being recognized. These songs are still being used in commercials, films and television episodes. Legacy soundtracks such as those for *Purple Rain* or *Footloose* continue to log ranks in music industry sales tracking. And, as remakes and sequels of films from the 1980s are brought out, interest surges in the music that made the originals such big hits.

One of the other great things about music from the Decade of Excess is that much of it had lyrics that were either misunderstood or left widely open to interpretation. Is Billy Idol's *Dancing With Myself* a commentary on the youth of the day or is it about the act of self-pleasure? Is The Human League's *Don't You Want Me* a song about a breakup or an unhealthy, ongoing relationship. I mean, perennial wedding staple *Every Breath You Take* by The Police is not a romantic tune and is instead a song from the point of view of a stalker. And Bruce Springsteen's *Born in the USA* is actually a harsh criticism of the United States and the way veterans were treated, but it's trotted out as a song of pride for the USA every Fourth of July. Oops.

Keeping this in mind, it only made sense to create an anthology of crime stories based on some of the most fun, "poppy" hits of the 1980s. I gathered together 11 extremely talented crime writers and asked them to put their own spin on some of these classic songs that were such an integral part of my (and thousands of others) childhood. Each also has a healthy dose of humor to keep the lightheartedness of the feel of songs of the era, but let's not forget that sometimes those songs harbored a dark side. These stories are no different.

I hope you enjoy these supremely fresh, choice, tasty tales. There isn't a bogus one among them. As if! Not one is grody to the max. And, if you understood all that, welcome fellow '80s fan. If you didn't, there's no doubt you'll still find these stories to be most bodacious.

J. Alan Hartman
Editor
June 2025

# *Sappho's Girl*
## *Linda Kay Hardie*

Looking back, I'm pretty sure everything started to unravel when Rick Springfield's song *Jesse's Girl* came up on my phone's playlist. At the time, I was working on editing a 140-year-old public domain translation of the poem by Greek poet Sappho known as Poem 31. Sometimes it's titled by its first line, which in 'my' translation is *Like a God, He Seems to Me.*

*Whoa. TMI all at once. I'm lost already.*

*Antwon, you listen too fast.*

*Say what?*

*Let me tell it my way, my friend.*

*All right, all right. Writers!*

I lived in a small city in Northern Nevada and taught at a nearby small private college. That semester I had two sections of Ancient and Medieval Cultures and two of English comp. The English department chair told me there was no budget for me to use a copyrighted translation of Sappho's poem in my classes. I pointed out to him that this is the entire purpose of using textbooks, and I would have my students buy the latest translation (from Gillian Spraggs or Guy Davenport) through the college bookstore (now run by a for-profit major corporate bookstore chain), but he was adamant. So there I was, taking out all the thee's and thou's and weird spellings like gaz'd and glanc'd, and trying to make this wonderful lesbian love poem "relevant" to my 19-year-old, short-attention-spanned students. I could use it in both the humanities class (where I struggle to find women to focus on) and the English class.

Besides which, Sappho is a damned good poet, even in the worst translation. In a skilled one, she's amazing. Here's the first stanza in my edit of the 1883, rather clunky translation by Symonds:

"Like a god he seems to me, the blissful
Man who sits and gazes at you before him,
Close beside you sits, and in silence hears you
Silverly speaking..."

Sappho, from the island of Lesbos (*yes, that's where the word came from*), wrote love poems to women, and this was one of the best of all time.

Hearing Springfield's great '80s song about a cishet love triangle is when I realized I was in a much worse situation than Jesse, his "girl," and his best friend in the song. I was in a mash-up of *Jesse's Girl* and *Sappho 31*, where I was the Sappho narrator, loving another woman (who in the song would have been "Rick's" girlfriend) from afar. I was in a love pentacle, and this was untenable. Someone needed to die.

*Antwon!*

*What? I didn't say anything.*

*You rolled your eyes.*

*English majors and their big words! Now you're rolling your eyes. I know that untenable means something can't last because of major problems with it. Gay men read books, you know. But c'mon, don't leave us in suspenders.*

*Are you familiar with the song?*

*No. Not my era.*

*So the narrator, the "Rick" character, lusts after his best friend Jesse's girlfriend. And he has some pretty specific daydreams. In the song, it's not clear if anyone is actually cheating but "Rick" isn't far away.*

When I heard the song, it woke me to the fact that I'd been complacent too long. The "Jesse" in our situation didn't have any suspicions yet. But I did know that our "Ricky" and the girlfriend had started, shall we say, canoodling?

> *What's her name?*
>
> *She doesn't have one in the song. Let's call her Joanna.*
>
> *Why?*
>
> *I'm changing names to protect the innocent, as they used to say in that cop show on TV.*
>
> *Boy, you are old!*
>
> *You want to hear this or not?*
>
> *Lips. Sealed. Please?*

Meanwhile, Ricky's girlfriend, and I'll call her Tikki, was also unaware of the affair.

> *Why Tikki?*
>
> *For Rudyard Kipling's heroic mongoose Rikki-Tikki-Tavi. I've always loved that character. Don't give me that look. I'm an English geek. Sue me.*

To continue. The five of us were all adjuncts at the same small college, part of a group that met Thursday late afternoons at a Midtown bar to drink and laugh and dance to songs on the jukebox and eat appetizers and relax after a week of dealing with first-year students. Who, by the way, are now considered "clients" by the administration, clients who need to be placated and rewarded with good grades for their pricey investment. What happened to coming to college for an education? To, you know, *learn* things?

But I digress. Altogether there was usually around a baker's dozen of us. We met on Thursdays, because it was the end of the week for us, teaching-wise, so the bar didn't mind us taking over the place. We filled almost half the tables in the small bar called Inanna's. This particular day, Thursday the 13th, was the end of the week when I'd heard the "Jesse's Girl" song.

> *Wait! You're trying to pull a fast one on us!*

*What is it, Antwon?*

*I happen to know that Inanna is a Sumerian war goddess. And you know that, as a professor of ancient cultures. But a bar with that name?*

*So I changed the business names, too. This bar was a small business, owned by a pair of lesbians. Not actually a "gay" bar, but it was welcoming to everyone who was copacetic with everyone. And they probably would have called it that if they'd had a classical education. So?*

*Just wanted to set things straight. Go on.*

We were all drinking and doing our usual bitching about first-year students, since most of us taught required courses in English and humanities and math. Several of us represented multiple departments, since we were all paid by the class, so we taught as many classes as we could get each semester in as many departments as we were qualified for. Contract workers with no stability and absolutely no tenure. Ever.

That's when I realized that Jesse and Tikki were oblivious to their respective significant others' affair. I was flying solo because I had five classes that semester, which is too much work to be fair to a partner. At least that's my story and I'm sticking to it. Also, I'd broken up a few months back and was fighting an unrequited crush on Tikki. Life was complicated enough.

Turned out I was a bit wrong though. Tikki and I ended up meeting in the ladies' room several hours into our bacchanal. More of a revelry, actually. We did a lot of drinking and dancing, but no orgies.

But while I had come in for the usual bladder reason, apparently Tikki had come in to cry. Her eyes were red and she was splashing water on her face.

"Is it something I can help with?" I asked. I don't have the best social graces and tend to just put my foot into it. But Tikki was used to my bluntness.

"Sappho, I think Ricky's having an affair."

I nodded.

"You knew?"

"I figured it out a few days ago. I saw him and Joanna making cow eyes at each other in the mailroom. I kicked over a wastebasket to announce myself, and they leaped apart."

"And I was starting to think he was 'the one.' Mostly." Tears leaked out of her eyes and rolled down her cheeks.

I'm not a huggy sort of person, and I had a crush on this woman. Damn. *Pretend she's a stray cat*, I told myself firmly. I cautiously wrapped my arms around her and awkwardly patted her on the shoulder. She hugged me, then stepped away. I avoided her eyes and tilted my head toward the stalls. (I said I was awkward. And I had to pee.)

When I came out, Tikki was wiping her face with paper towels after splashing more water.

"Thanks." She blew her nose into the damp paper. "I guess it's better to know for sure."

I nodded.

"But what do I do now?" She straightened her back. In a stronger voice, she said, "I need to break it off with him. Now." And she scowled.

My opinion of her skyrocketed. She had gumption.

"Well," I said, unsure if I should voice the thought. To hell with it. "We could kill him."

"And her, too?"

I love gumption.

> *That's quite a leap.*
> *What is, Antwon?*
> *Going from being mad at someone to deciding to kill him.*
> *Yeah, I know. We did talk it over when we were clear-headed and not drunk.*

Tikki came over to my apartment the next day. I was burning sandalwood incense to calm down. I'd gone too far in the heat of the moment and possibly revealed too much about my background, in a way. I needed the mental clarity and emotional balance of sandalwood's warm, earthy aroma.

I had the front door open with the screen keeping the cats inside, so I wasn't surprised to hear a light tapping and "knock-knock" in Tikki's voice.

"Down, Fiona, Banshee." I shooed the cats away and opened the screen door. When Tikki stepped in, I closed the front door behind her. I certainly didn't want my nosy neighbors listening in on this conversation. Most of them had figured out I was a witch, but they weren't nasty neighbors, just nosy. Murder, though, would be a bridge too far.

"Beautiful cats." Tikki sat down cross-legged on the floor to pet the girls. They purred like small, idling UPS trucks and rubbed their cheek glands all over her. "What kind of cat are they?"

"They're Abyssinians. Very friendly, very smart, very athletic. Fii's color is ruddy and the Banshee's is fawn."

Tikki laughed. "They're wonderful! I understand Fiona the redhead, but Banshee?"

"Her pedigreed name is Bit O' Honey, and she was called Bito, but when I got her, she arrived on a flight from the breeder in North Carolina. When I picked her up at the shipping counter in the airport, I could hear her howling long before they ever brought her out."

She laughed again. "But she survived."

I chuckled. "That's more than I can say for the poor pedigreed Chihuahua that shared the airplane's baggage compartment with her. Already a high-strung breed, this poor critter was shivering from all those hours with her. And the Banshee is still a big talker."

"*The* Banshee?"

"It's more of a title than a name."

I sat down in my favorite chair and waved an arm to indicate another chair or the couch, but Tikki shook her head.

"I'm fine down here, if you don't mind." Fiona chose that moment to head-butt Tikki's chin, and we all laughed, we humans with our voices and the girls with their cat-grin squints.

And just like that, I felt awkward. I'm not good around people I don't know or trust yet, or in situations where I'm not in control, like I am in the classroom. Tikki continued to pet the cats.

Finally I spoke. "Uh, about last night..."

"I'm sorry," we said simultaneously.

"What?" we both said. And we laughed again.

"Me first." I waved my hand, as though I were a student. "I want to apologize for what I said last night. You know, about... murder?"

"No. I was going to apologize for that," Tikki said. "See, what you don't know is that I didn't realize how toxic this relationship was until I discovered he was cheating on me. And after Ricky went to bed last night, I stayed up almost until dawn, writing in my journal about everything I hadn't had the guts to admit to myself until your... suggestion last night."

"Everything?" I whispered. The tone of her voice made it sound awfully intimate. "If you want to tell me, that is. I don't mean to pry."

"No, it's okay." Tikki looked at the cats, and I thought she wanted to get up but was too polite to shove the cats off her legs.

"Shoo, girls," I said, waving an "away" gesture at them. They gave me a quick glare, but scampered to the back of the apartment where the sun shone through the window this time of day.

Tikki stood up, brushing fur off her clothes. She sat on the couch and stared down at her hands clasped in her lap. She spoke without looking over at me.

"I moved in with Ricky five weeks ago, and he changed. Right away. But I didn't acknowledge it to myself until yesterday, right before our gathering at Inanna's, when I heard him talking on his phone in an intimate tone to Joanna. I realized I hadn't heard that tone from him since I'd given notice on my apartment and brought all my stuff over."

She was quiet for several minutes.

"Let me get us some wine," I said.

Tikki looked up at me and nodded. I awkwardly patted her shoulder on my way to the kitchen, and I brought back two glasses of a nice Argentinian Torrontes, my new favorite white.

She took a couple of sips and asked me what it was. I told her and she smiled and sipped some more.

"So once you had nowhere to go, he showed his true colors?" I said.

"Yes. I found myself doing all the cooking and cleaning. I was constantly picking up his dirty underwear and socks from all over the house. I did the laundry. At first I thought it was sweet that he wanted to do the shopping with me, but as I wrote in my journal, it dawned on me that he was keeping an eye on me." She paused to sip more wine.

"Why?" I drank, too.

"He didn't want me talking to people too much. And he wanted to choose what I bought. I like chicken and fish, bur Ricky prefers beef and hamburger, so that's what we ate. That sort of thing."

"Isolating you."

Tikki nodded.

I let her gather her thoughts, but after a few minutes I asked her the big question.

"Did he hit you?"

She sat silent for a minute. "Not until last night. When we got home, he yelled at me for staying so long in the bathroom and accused me of 'conspiring' with you." Tikki looked embarrassed. "But that's the only time! And he was drunk."

"Tikki, don't make excuses for him. Hitting is hitting. No one 'makes' someone else hit them. Believe me, I know."

I put my hand on hers. Then I stood up.

"I'll be right back." I walked to the kitchen and came back with a fresh bottle of Torrontes and poured us both another glass.

"Tikki, I didn't come out of the closet, even to myself, until after my divorce."

"But you were in your 30s then, weren't you?"

"Mid 30s. And I'd repressed my identity so deep that I didn't even know I was doing it. The 'gay lifestyle' was not something I could even entertain. My parents tried not to be bigoted, but they were in many ways." I took another drink of wine. And then a deep breath. At this point, I hadn't told anyone these details. Not even my divorce attorney.

"My mom made comments like, 'Ugh, how can you listen to Elton John? He gives me the creeps, thinking about him and…Ugh. You know.' I knew. And I knew that my parents could never like—let alone love—someone like that. I never even let myself think I was that someone."

Tikki poured the last of the wine into my glass.

"Only my divorce attorney knows all these details." I took another sip of the wine. "I was married 11 years. The abuse started in year two. Initially it was only verbal. Shouting, calling me stupid or crazy, giving me the silent treatment for days because of an imagined slight. I thought everything was my fault, partly because he told me so and partly because (as I see now, looking back) I was still trying to be the good girl who wasn't queer. The third year he started hitting."

My glass was empty again. So was the bottle. I looked up to see Tikki looking at me with kind eyes.

'You don't have to tell me," she said.

"I think you need to know."

"Okay. Thank you for sharing. I see how hard this is, but we've each had three glasses of wine and it's just barely lunch time. I could fix us sandwiches. I think we both need to boost our blood sugar."

"Let's do it together."

We worked well as a team fixing grilled cheese and turkey sandwiches on sourdough. I collected the ingredients and pointed out equipment (skillet, spatula, knife) while she put it all together. She even sprinkled a little garlic powder on the buttered outsides before grilling the sandwiches. I made a pitcher of iced tea, and we switched to that when we returned to the living room.

*Wow, girl. I never would have guessed. I'm so sorry for you.*

*Thanks, Antwon. I told her the rest, how even though I knew how abuse works, I still thought that in this case it was my fault. It's so hard to see the gaslighting for what it is when you're inside its bubble. And the hitting always seemed spontaneous, spur of the moment, so it was easy for him to convince me that he wouldn't do it if I didn't say the wrong thing or disrespect him. All the usual shit. There was nothing exceptional about my abuse story. Until the end.*

"How did you get out?" Tikki asked. "You divorced him, right? You didn't... you know... kill him?"

I could see a mixture of fear and hope in her eyes.

"A final and unthinkable act of abuse finally woke me up," I said. "I walked into his home office one morning. I wasn't trying to be sneaky, but I was wearing woolly socks and the carpet was thick. I saw him kick Sundance across the room. He was my fawn aby boy."

She gasped.

"Sundance hit the closet door with a thud. I shrieked. The cat leaped up and ran from the room. I could see realization dawning in the fucking bastard that he'd made a fatal mistake. Only figuratively, alas, but if looks could actually kill, I would be in jail. But after a moment, I turned and ran after my kitty."

"Sundance, was he all right?"

"Yes. As soon as I determined that, I started to pack. The bastard initially yelled and threatened me, but when that didn't work, he groveled and pleaded. He tried to gaslight me into believing that somehow he didn't kick the cat, that somehow Sundance just ran into the closet door by himself."

We both sat silently, drinking tea. Tikki excused herself to go to the bathroom. I collected plates and glasses and took them to the kitchen. Tikki walked in.

"So how does this lead to murder?" she asked.

"I'm tired of abusive men getting away with near-murder and actual murder. My lawyer provided evidence of his abuse of me, but his got it thrown out. I know a woman who killed herself in similar circumstances."

"But still. Ricky only hit me one time."

"That's just the start. We've got to nip this in the bud."

So we decided to do it. But neither of us had any real idea how. We were talking about murder mysteries we'd read and movies we'd seen when a loud knock at my door interrupted us. It was Jesse. He had a black eye.

"Sappho, um, could I come in? I wanted to talk to you, because you're such a good listener. Oh. I didn't know you had company already."

I'd motioned for him to come in.

"No, it's okay," Tikki said. "I was just leaving."

"Uh, if you could stay? I'm, well, I'm embarrassed, but I need a woman's point of view." Jesse sat in the chair on the other side of the couch.

"Sure," I said. "Would you like a drink? Iced tea? Wine? Scotch?"

"Uh. Yes. I'd love scotch, but isn't it kind of early?"

Tikki and I looked at each other and chuckled. Jesse stared.

"Sorry," Tikki said. "But it's been that kind of day. We've been drinking wine."

"No worries," I said. "I'll get you a scotch. It's rocks, isn't it?"

Jesse nodded.

He took a sip when I brought the drink. Then he looked at us, and drank the whole thing. He held onto the glass, poking at the ice cubes with a finger.

"Joanna punched me," he said without preamble.

We both gasped.

"Why?" I asked.

"I don't know. She did it this morning right when I got up. She'd been up for a while, but I drank more than usual last night, so I felt lousy and stayed in bed. I was sitting on the edge of the bed wishing for the room to stop spinning when she came in and picked a fight with me. I thought things were getting better. Joanna and I haven't fought in almost a week."

My eyes met Tikki's. Were Ricky and Joanna the perfect couple for each other?

"And she punched you in the eye?" Tikki asked.

Jesse nodded.

"Does she hit you a lot?" I asked.

Jesse gulped the dregs of his drink, mostly scotch-flavored melted ice. "What do you mean by a lot?"

A question that answered itself, alas. Jesse turned out to be a part of our new club. I poured him another scotch while Tikki made him a grilled sandwich after he told us he hadn't eaten at all today. He'd dressed and fled their apartment, then drove around town for hours until he thought of talking to me. Joanne had accused him of ogling other women at the bar. He hadn't been, and I'd noticed that. I pay attention to these things now.

Tikki and I let him in our plans, which we expanded to include Joanna. I would love to play poker with Jesse, because I could see everything going on in his head flash across his face. Denial, anger, bargaining, depression, and acceptance. Just like the stages of grief.

Over the next few weeks, the three of us followed our victims to learn their schedules, where they met to cheat. We plotted ways we could kill them. We started out with wild ideas, like calling the police on them and having the SWAT team kill them. Or building a pipe bomb and having it blow up a boat they were on. These unworkable plans were nonsense from the beginning. The police wouldn't kill them because Ricky and Joanna wouldn't pose any danger. We didn't know how to make any kind of a bomb, and they didn't have a boat.

We even recycled some Wile E. Coyote ideas. Dropping something heavy on them. Yeah, right. Running over them with a large truck. Besides the fact that hit and run is easily solved, we all had small, cheap, beat-up cars which probably wouldn't even be able to drive away from the crime. And all of us had maxed-out credit cards, so we couldn't rent a truck. And how do you return a rental truck with busted headlights and blood on the bumper?

We met at my apartment two weeks later.

"What now?" Jesse asked. He had a new black eye and his left index finger was in a splint. He only shook his head when we asked what happened.

"How about poison?" Tikki said. "I read a crime story recently about a woman who poisoned her abusive ex-husband by using oleander leaves instead of bay leaves to make spaghetti sauce, and then her ex stole what he thought was her lunch out of the company fridge at work. She got away with it in the story, although I think she was going to poison another co-worker who figured it out. That probably wouldn't have been a good idea."

"How about putting a curse on them?" Jesse said. "You're a witch, Sappho. Can you do something?"

"Fuck. I'm not supposed to be killing anyone anyway, since I'm a Wiccan. Our only religious rule is the Rede, which says "Do as ye will, an ye harm none.'"

"Oh!" Tikki looked shocked. "Will you lose your soul or something?"

"No. It means that whatever energy I put out into the universe bounces back to me."

"Let's think of something else then," Jesse said.

We tried. When it came to murder, none of us had the least bit of imagination.

"Well," I finally said. "I actually do have a spell book that has curses in it. Let's take a look." I trotted to my bedroom bookcase to get it, a super-thick encyclopedia of 5,000 spells of all kinds. I bought it from the discount table at our local bookstore chain years ago.

We perused the table of contents. Most of the spells weren't evil or damaging ones. Lots of money and luck spells, love spells, all that. Spells to attract or repel people. We found "impotence" in the index and focused on those. It was in the dark magic section, and we carefully looked through this part. Besides, an impotence spell wouldn't screw up my karma too much.

I had the ingredients on hand. Certain herbs, innocent by themselves. Certain stones. Particular incenses. A regular egg from the grocery store. Some other stuff I won't mention. And I won't give the incantation or instructions. We charged two pieces of tumbled obsidian with this spell, and Tikki and Jesse put the stones under their partners' pillows that night.

The next day we gathered everyone at Jesse's apartment. Ricky and Joanna squirmed in their chairs on opposite sides of the living room. Both were scowling slightly, looking very much like they were feeling bowel cramps.

I had no idea whether the spell would work, nor what it would even do if it did. But I did enjoy seeing them uncomfortable.

Jesse spoke first. "Joanna, you've abused me long enough. I'm not going to be your victim anymore. You need to pack up your things and get out of here today."

She blanched. "Abuse? Me? What? You're the abuser!"

"What about my broken finger? You grabbed me and pulled it backward until it broke." Jesse held up his splinted finger.

"I was defending myself when you tried to hit me!"

"I was sitting on the toilet when you came in, screamed at me, then broke it without provocation," Jesse said. "And my black eye?"

"Self-defense."

"You don't have as much as a broken fingernail, Joanna," I said.

"Ricky," Tikki said.

He jumped in his chair. "What?"

"I'm moving out. You've hit me enough."

"But I never—"

"Yes, you did."

Ricky stood up. "I'll throw you out. I'm going to change the locks so you can't get in. You can't get any of your stuff."

"My sister and her husband should have it all moved out by now. I gave her my key."

Ricky sank back into the chair.

"And there's more," I said. "We know that you two are cheating. Did you see the obsidian stones under your pillows last night? I've put a curse on you. You'll never be able to have satisfactory sex again. Especially with each other."

Joanna and Ricky began shouting. I couldn't tell what they were saying, but it didn't matter. I didn't care.

*So is that it? Is that the end of the story? Did they break up?*

*No. We did hear through the grapevine that they actually were having sexual problems. And a friend of mine, another witch, texted me to say they'd contacted him to take the curse off. He asked what I would like him to do. He was a good friend.*

The rest of it we saw on the local TV news. Ricky and Joanna were found, unconscious, amid the ruins of a display bed in one of the big chain furniture stores. Naked, except for lurid body paint in gaudy shades of blue, orange, green, and red, "in satanic symbols," the news reporter said.

They were discovered by the store's assistant manager, who called the cops. The cops first called the paramedics, then had a team of photographers document all of the symbols painted on Ricky and Joanna's bodies. Both had awakened in time for the photographers. Then they were arrested (being conscious was required so the cops could read them their rights). The paramedics confirmed that the two had simply been knocked out when the plywood fake bed display crashed under their weight during their, uh, "passionate sex acts."

The TV news team got there in time to get footage of the body art as well, which they showed on the news report. Blurring a few bits, of course. The two suspects were taken to Nevada Mental Health on Galleti Way for a 72-hour mental health hold.

> *So now you know the whole story, Antwon. The three of us fled Nevada in embarrassment. Fortunately, curses are not actually against the law and can't be proven in court to exist. I don't even know if I really cursed them. But we didn't want to take chances. Tikki realized she was in love with me and that she must be bisexual. Jesse said he was going to move to Alaska and become a crabber on a boat, where he would be out at sea for weeks at a time, until he discovered that there's not much call for them anymore what with crab shortages due to over-harvesting and climate change. So he came with us, as you well know.*
>
> *Yes. Give me a hug, my big teddy bear!*
>
> *And the moral of the story is that there are more queer people than society realizes. Ever since I came out, I've always thought most people are at least a little bit queer in some way, and this proves it.*

# *Motivation*
## *Steve Shrott*

I opened the door to our tiny apartment and shouted. "I got it. I got it."

Cheryl looked at me concerned. "Not the fungus again."

"No, no, the job. I got the job."

Her blue eyes opened wide. "At the accounting firm?"

"Yes."

"That's terrific, Tim. We'll be able to save up for the wedding now." Cheryl moved close and gave me a big kiss. Unfortunately, her aim was a little off and she got my nose. She really needed new glasses.

My love released me, her brow crinkling. "And there's no fungus?"

"All Clear. You know I think this job is gonna be great. I'm starting off as a clerk but once the boss see's how devoted I am, I'm sure I'll be promoted."

"It's 9 to 5, right?"

I nodded. I thought that would make everything okay. But as I looked at her still concerned face, I realized it wouldn't. "Not this again, honey. It's about me working the night shift at the hot dog truck isn't it?"

Cheryl removed a tissue from her pocket and wiped her eyes. "That girl blew a kiss at you."

"I told you it wasn't a kiss. She was just trying to cool down her fries. Look honey, I know I have amazing dimples and I look hot in a Speedo, even though that crazy doctor says I'm 30 pounds overweight, but the thing is, you're my lady. You have to stop being so jealous."

"I know." She went in for another kiss. I moved my head up so she'd get my lips this time.

The next morning I tumbled out of bed excited about my first day. Cheryl made me a hearty breakfast of oatmeal, and bacon and eggs. Then I hopped into my Honda and drove downtown.

I was thrilled to be working again after the hot dog truck fiasco.

The job started off okay but I was barely getting by. I was in charge of relish but I had dreams of moving up to some of the other condiments. Sad to say, Randy the boss wouldn't let me. Then he started taking credit for all my great ideas—like having three dogs in a hamburger bun. I called it 'Tim's Triple Play.' Not bad huh? But he changed it to 'Randy's Cheap Sex on a Bun,' which he painted on the side of the truck. The only problem was that some kids scraped off the 'on a bun' part—which explains why the police closed the business down two days later.

Then I heard about this clerk job and I knew the tide was gonna turn and things were going to go my way.

I parked and got out of my car. It was wonderful walking down the street feeling the vibrant energy of all the other folks who worked nine to five jobs. I gotta tell you my blood was really pumping.

I entered the tall steel and glass building that housed ASD Accounting—thirty-five minutes early by the way-and the receptionist led me to my office. It was glorious, an L-shaped desk and loads of wall space where I could hang pictures of my relatives. They were proud pacifists like me—all the way from my great great granddaddy, Titus, to my father, Alowishes. Like them I did not believe in conflict. The only time I raised a fist was to give someone a fist bump. Unfortunately, the Dawdler Twins at North Western High thought I was going to punch them, and a day later the doctor had to move my nose back to its original position. Or thereabouts.

I got word the boss wanted to see me and immediately marched to his office. I sat down in front of his huge desk as he moved documents around. I have to say he was a bit imposing with the scar on the right side of his face and the missing finger.

"Welcome aboard, Tim. I know we hired you as a clerk, but I was so impressed with your interview I'd like to promote you to Manager of

Global Interoffice Affairs—with a pay raise."

I put my hand on my chest. "Thank you Mr. Williams." My life was certainly turning around. I had an ear to ear smile which wasn't easy with the new nose position.

"Let's get to your first project. Lately I've noticed some irregularities in the work of one of our CPA's, Horus Baminsky. I've given him many opportunities to improve but his work is still mediocre at best. I need you to tell him to do better or he'll be fired."

I started breathing heavy. I thought it was going to be a simple clerk job like sorting papers, much like I sorted the relish into sweet, tangy, and 'wow, call the smoke jumpers my tonsils are on fire.'

"Horus has a lot of potential. Not YOU potential, but potential. I think this will motivate him to do better.  I've learned a lot about what makes people tick from my time in that Mexican prison. Trumped up charges of course."

"Mexican Prison?"

"Yes, I was amongst the most sadistic people imaginable, crazy murderers who would do anything to anyone for a peso. Lots of fighting going on. And so bloody."

"Fighting? Bloody?" My hand started to tremble hearing this so I put my other hand on top. But then it started to tremble too. "Uh couldn't we just say that Horus needs to improve his work a smidge or he'll have to consider…other opportunities?"

Williams thought a moment then smiled. "Great idea. We'll call it the Tim Crenshaw Approach. It's softer, gentler. Well done, my boy."

I left the office feeling good. I was a company man now and I had a boss who liked my ideas. What could be better?

Of course I was a little hesitant about giving this poor man the bad news. I wasn't good at that. I once ate all of my Aunt Goldie's Strawberry Shortcake instead of telling her she accidently used red buttons instead of strawberries. Unfortunately, later I found out they weren't buttons, they were her 'Go Now' pills, and I spent two days in the washroom.

Horus sat in his office, eating a cheese sandwich at his desk. I was about to talk to him, but then he stood up. I froze. The man was a muscled giant.

His arms were enormous with tattoos of skulls and crossbones and his shoes were the size of three half-foot long wieners laid end to end. Well actually I guess that's eighteen inches, but I was hungry. My heart pounded but somehow I got out words, "Hey Horus, I'm Tim, I work with Mr. Williams. How are you?"

He grunted which I took for 'good,' but it could have meant, I will grind you into a tiny powder with my pinky finger.

"Mr. Williams thinks your, uh, great, but he wonders if you could, uh, do a teensy weensy better in your work."

He moved close so that we were almost nose to nose. Of course with my nose situation, he was still a little to the left. I could feel his very hot breath on my face. It was like I was in a sauna with the thermostat set to purgatory.

"And if I don't do better?" He lifted one of his enormous meat hook hands and formed it into a fist.

"Well, uh, you might have to find, uh, other…opportunities."

Yes, I told him that right to his face. That's due to my courage, bravery, and racing the hell out of there right after I said it. I ran down the hall and into my office banging the door shut, and pushing my desk against it. I was hyperventilating so much I had to squeeze my stress ball about a hundred times. It exploded. Guess it couldn't take the stress either. Then I looked up at the picture of great great granddaddy Titus to see if I could imagine what his input would be. I think he would have just said, "run faster and push a lot more furniture against the door."

I eventually calmed down, and since there were no other assignments, I spent the time introducing myself to everyone. They seemed nice and no one looked like they would steal someone's genius idea for a hot dog sandwich.

At five o'clock I went for a drink at The Corral, a nearby bar. It was a small place and very dark. I could barely find my jumbo shrimp on the plate. Eventually I located them behind the jumbo meatballs. Sometimes eating can really be a scavenger hunt. As I ate, I thought about the job. I hoped the rest of my assignments wouldn't involve conflict like at the hot dog truck. I remember one time Randy accused me of stealing a pickle and eating it during work hours. We didn't have any fancy-dancy video surveillance so he just had Pablo smell me. Luckily, he reported there was no evidence of dill.

I was thrilled that though the first assignment had been tough, I had accomplished it with flying colors. It seemed like nine to five was truly a better fit for me.

I was all set to go home when I heard a sweet voice call my name.

"Tim. Tim Crenshaw?"

I looked up to see Betty Nashman, an old girlfriend of mine, her perfect face smiling down on me like an angel. In high school I thought she was the one. She gave me a hug and a big kiss on the lips. Though I felt guilty about it, I gave her high marks for accuracy. Right on the mouth, first time. Of course I made sure Betty knew that I had a girlfriend. But then she talked about her boyfriend Dan, and I felt more relaxed. We chatted about the old days and sometime having a couple's thing.

After she left, I realized I couldn't tell Cheryl about meeting Betty. She would read all kinds of things into it that weren't there. I looked at my watch and realized I'd better get home before she called in the FBI, CIA and Interpol.

* * *

The next afternoon, Cheryl sat at her best friend Didi's kitchen table chewing a cookie. Didi sipped a glass of wine and with her other hand stroked her bushy eyebrows. "You look upset, Cheryl. What's wrong?"

"Tim came home at seven-o-two last night. He should have been home by six-o-seven. It's a nine to five job."

"What did he say?"

"He claimed things came up."

Didi shook her head. "What could come up? A flood? Locusts? A Chihuahua giving him a dirty look and Tim hiding in a closet?"

"It's that lady at the hot dog truck all over again."

Didi chugged the rest of her wine down. "I know what we have to do."

"What?"

"Put a tracker on his car—find out what he does, where he goes."

Cheryl swallowed the rest of her cookie then leaned forward. "That seems a bit much."

"By now the man could have seduced the entire secretarial pool as well as the lunch lady in the cafeteria."

"Aren't those usually about eighty with blue hair?"

"Men like Tim don't care about a woman's age or hair color. They just want to get into her meatloaf if you know what I mean."

* * *

A few days later Williams called me into the office. He had a stern look on his face. "We got problems, Tim."

"Oh?"

"I know you gave it your all, but Horus' work has not improved since your little chat." He spread his hands. "We need to do something."

I didn't like where this was going. "Look, I don't feel comfortable having another talk with Horus. He didn't seem too happy last time."

"Once again Tim you are absolutely right. Talking is of no use. It's gone too far already. I need you to…show him we mean business."

"What?"

"Rough him up a little."

I felt every part of my body start to shake causing my jockey shorts to slide down around my ankles. "The thing is I, uh, don't have the arm strength for something like that. I need three people at the gym to help me do a push up."

"I understand where you're coming from, Tim. But I have something that will help you strategically."

He reached under his desk and pulled out a baseball bat. "Now don't worry, you don't have to knock him out or anything. Just a bop or two to make him understand the situation."

"Mr. Williams, I can't do that."

"I know this is kind of against your principles."

"Yes, and Horus is also very big."

"Right. But how would your girlfriend feel about you losing your promotion and maybe your job because you're not willing to do what it takes?"

"I don't think she'd feel too good. You know we're planning a wedding and I promised that we'd save for it and…"

"What do you think she'd say about you being out with another woman?"

"What?"

"Just a question."

"She would definitely not like that."

Williams opened a drawer and removed a large brown envelope. He tore it open and took out several photos.

I gasped. One was a picture of the ex I had met yesterday kissing me. Another was of us in a hug, and though I didn't notice it at the time, her hand was definitely in an area where a woman, who's not your girlfriend, should be visiting.

"Where did you get those?"

He shrugged. "It was on my desk this morning. I certainly wouldn't want to have to share these with your girlfriend."

This was unbelievable. He was going to blackmail me. I couldn't let Cheryl see these photos even though nothing happened. And if he fired me, we wouldn't have the money for any kind of wedding. As the French say, Je suis screwed.

* * *

Cheryl sat in the passenger seat of Didi's ten year old Volkswagen with the bent fender. In her hands she held a GPS tracker.

Didi made a sharp turn, the wheels squealing. "I'm thinking you made a mistake going out with Tim in the first place."

Cheryl nodded. "I've thought about that. I mean I love Tim, but it bothers me that he's so passive like the rest of his family. I think a relationship needs conflict sometimes. I always fantasized about meeting someone adventurous like James Bond or Indiana Jones."

"I always liked Hannibal Lector, although his dietary habits greatly violated the Weight Watcher point system. Didi started to laugh, then pointed to the tracker. "Look it's blinking."

* * *

That night wearing a moustache, and dark glasses, I followed Horus into The Warwick Bar near the office. In my clarinet case, I had the bat instead of my clarinet, which I played pretty well considering I only knew two notes. Of course that may explain why I'd never been asked to perform solos at my high school assemblies.

The place was pretty lively other than the six men with their heads on the table passed out. I sat in the back and ordered the hard stuff--cranberry juice (it could do a number on my acid reflux.) as I watched Horus.

After many beers, he stumbled out of the bar. I followed. It was raining like crazy and I slipped a bit.

I looked around the streets and saw that they were deserted. I figured no one would be out in this weather. A good thing for me.

I unzipped the case and took out the bat. Horus was now waiting in front of the bus stop. I guess he didn't want to drive due to being drunk. I felt bad thumping a man who was so socially conscious, but there were important matters at stake here. I crept into the empty bus shelter just behind the stop, then slowly stepped toward Horus. I lifted the bat high into the air and started shaking all over. It made sense. I was about to do something my relatives would shoot me in the gonads for if they weren't all pacifists.

* * *

Didi parked on the street near The Warwick. They were about to don their sombreros and fake noses when they saw Tim walking out of the bar. Cheryl noticed Tim's case. "That's his clarinet. What's he doing with that?"

"Some men like to seduce the ladies with music."

"He only knows two notes."

"With the right lady you only need one."

They watched as Tim took the bat out of the case, and entered the bus shelter. When he moved toward the man, and lifted the bat into the air, Cheryl's face turned white. "W-W-What's h-h-he doing?"

Didi shrugged. "My uneducated guess is that he's about to knock the shit out that dude."

My perspiring hands held the bat tightly about to smash it into Horus. The adrenaline poured through me like Aunt Goldie's strawberry shortcake. Everything seemed to be happening in slow motion.

But then pre-whack, I stopped.

I just couldn't do it. It wasn't in me, no matter what the repercussions were to my life. I felt relieved for a moment. But then Horus whipped around. When he saw me with the bat, he became enraged. I'd never seen anyone that angry since my granddaddy discovered I lied and told everyone he received the Purple Heart for saving his platoon. He was disgusted.

I was frozen, couldn't move. Horus was a step away now as I struggled to get the hell out of there.

Finally, I broke free. I moved to the left of the bus stop to avoid him, but he moved to the left. Then I went to the right of the stop, and he went to the right. It was like we were dancing. I have to say for a big man he was very light on his feet.

Suddenly he started slipping on the watery pavement--his legs going in all different directions. Then he seemed to get confused and his head slammed into the bus stop with a cracking sound. He whirled around and dropped to the ground, his eyes closed, his face all banged up, and bloody.

* * *

Cheryl and Didi covered their eyes when Tim held the bat over the big man, too frightened to watch. Moments later they heard a cracking sound and had to look.

They saw the man fell to the ground.

Cheryl's eyes opened wide and her mouth quivered. "H-H-How could Tim do this? H-H-He's a pacifist."

"Apparently not so much."

* * *

I couldn't believe he had hit the bus stop. I knelt down beside him. "Horus, Horus, can you hear me?"

His eyes flickered.

I breathed a sigh of relief. He was alive, thank goodness. I called 911. A few moments later an ambulance took him to the hospital.

The next day Williams applauded as I walked into his office. "Fantastic job with Horus, Tim. You really gave it to him. Apparently he made it to the hospital somehow, but he's in terrible shape. I think he'll definitely be a little more motivated now that he sees what you're capable of."

"I didn't do anything."

"Nonsense, my boy. You are a natural. I knew I'd hired the right man for the job. I pity to think what you would have done to those guys in that Mexican prison."

"His injuries had nothing to do with me."

"I love it. You don't even want to take credit for a job well done. You are a real find."

That night I went to the hospital to visit Horus. His eyes were closed and he had bandages wrapped around his head. Tubes fed into his body.

I knew he couldn't hear me, but I needed a way to assuage my guilt. "Hey Horus, I'm sorry about what happened to you. I feel bad for the part I played in this. I hope you get well very…"

Suddenly his eyes snapped open and he squeaked out words.

"You did this. I saw you with that bat. You were the weasel who was going to fire me too. I'm going to get even with you, make no mistake." Then his eyes shut and he seemed to go back to sleep. I figured it was a good time to leave if I wanted to keep all my body parts.

* * *

Cheryl and Didi walked down the long hospital hallway. Didi shook her head. "Why are we doing this?"

"We have to make amends."

"But Tim is the one who thwacked him."

"He's my boyfriend. Maybe I did something to make him do this."

"Fine."

They entered Horus' room and Cheryl sat down in the chair beside the bed. She started talking to an unconscious Horus. "I'm so sorry for what my boyfriend did to you. I don't know what got into him."

Didi, still standing by the door, whispered to Cheryl. "Maybe Tim's having a midlife crisis. Some men buy flashy cars. Tim beats up people."

Cheryl shrugged, then grabbed Horus' enormous hand and held it. "I will make this up to you any way I can."

Cheryl didn't see it, but Horus smiled for a moment.

*  *  *

I was up all night. Cheryl, as usual, slept like a log.

In the morning, I headed to the kitchen and had coffee. I swear I saw Horus looking in the window. I shivered. Of course it must have been my imagination working over time. I've been under a lot of stress lately as you can imagine. And that's when it occurred to me that maybe, just maybe, I had to get out of this job. I wasn't going to tell Cheryl anything about it. She was already upset with me last night for some reason. Wouldn't talk to me. I guess I've done a few bad things lately like not cleaning the tub after I took a bath.

The real problem with me quitting was that I had started paying for the rental of a hall that she'd loved, for our wedding. I wanted to surprise her with it, but I needed at least a few more weeks' salary to finish.

Three days later Horus returned to the office still bandaged up. I, of course, kept my distance, although hiding in the ladies washroom might not have been the most manly way to do that.

I went to see Williams in his office. He was sitting behind his desk making notes.

"Hey superstar. What's on your mind?"

"I wondered if I could go back to being just a clerk. I'm not sure I'm up to the challenge of this position."

"You can't leave now Tim. We're on the right track. For the first few days back, Horus did fantastic work even with his current issues. Unfortunately, now I see he's starting to falter again."

I knew where this was going. "Look that's it. I am not going to do anything else to this poor man. I will explain the pictures to my girlfriend if I have to."

Williams shook his head. "I was wrong to do that to you, Tim. But the problem now is that the payroll system has a virus and for some strange reason it only affects Horus' account. I know Horus is not that fond of you at the moment, and I'm sure he'll think you had something to do with this. Hopefully that won't cause any issues for you."

I started breathing heavy but managed to calm myself down. "I don't care what you say, I am not going to touch that bat again."

Williams held up his hand. "No, of course not, I wouldn't expect you to. It has gone way beyond that. He simply doesn't understand we are just trying to motivate him. No, we must go in another direction."

Williams reached into his pocket and pulled out a gun.

I felt dizzy.

"Now, don't get nervous. I just want you to give him a little flesh wound on his leg, arm and maybe shoulder. This helped Demetre, my roomy in prison, learn he should call me, sir, not doodles."

I stared at him a moment, then just walked out and went home. I had had it. This guy was crazy. I even called up Randy to see if he would hire me back. He said no, he didn't need me. He had changed the sandwich name to Randy's Triple Play, and it was doing well in his new food truck—especially since he added another dog. I told him that it didn't work with the name. Four dogs would be quadruple, not triple. But logic never seemed to be Randy's strong suit. He was a member of The Flat Earth Society and always rubbed 'sticky stuff' on his shoes so he wouldn't fall off the edge of the world.

I headed home. Cheryl was out which was good since all I felt like doing was going to bed and trying to forget everything that had happened. As I was about to lay down, I noticed a note on the bedside table. It read, "Cheryl, you are a wonder. Every part of your body is like a symphony and last night I played Beethoven's Fifth. I'm glad you found the bandages erotic. Also thanks for drying my socks. I'll pick them up tomorrow." It was signed Horus.

My heart beat a mile a minute as I raced downstairs to the dryer. I opened the door and saw my clothes intermixed with a man's socks that I'd never seen before. I pulled them out. At that moment, it all came together. Horus had gotten even with me like he said he would--in the worst possible way, making love to my girl.  I cried, wetting the socks again. Cheryl will probably be mad about that too.

Moments later, a strange thought entered my mind. I made a few calls, then headed over to the office.

* * *

Williams sat behind his desk as usual.

"I thought it over. Give me the gun."

"Now you're thinking right." He handed me the pistol. "Go to it. Maybe this will finally knock some sense into Horus."

I couldn't believe I was actually holding a firearm in my hands. It gave me the heebie-jeebies, but I had to go through with this. I adjusted the position of the gun, then aimed it at Williams.

"You did all this."

"What?"

"I called my ex and got her to confess that you paid her to bump into me, and then hired someone to take pictures of us together at the restaurant. You also wrote that note about Horus sleeping with my girlfriend. I have to say it was a nice touch with the socks."

"What are you talking about?"

"I saw Horus' notes on a tax file when I visited him in his office. That's not his writing on the letter to Cheryl, it's yours." I took the socks out of my pocket and lobbed them onto his desk. "And these aren't Horus'. His shoes are overly large so he wouldn't wear normal size socks."

At that moment, Horus entered the office. I had already explained everything on the phone to him. He gave me a high-five, then I handed him the gun. As I headed toward the door I heard Williams begging. "Don't shoot. I was only trying to motivate you guys."

* * *

Cheryl and Didi sat at the bar in The Warwick sipping their wines. Cheryl had a big smile on her face.

"I'm not sure why you're so happy. You just saw your boyfriend beat the crap out of some dude."

"I was upset at first, but then I thought about it. I kind of like the new Tim. He's more complex than I thought."

"Complex? The man's a thug."

"Not that I condone what he did. But maybe that guy deserved it. Maybe he was a crook or something."

Didi rolled her eyes. "Yeah, Tim's a superhero all right. He walloped a guy who might have committed the terrible crime of taking up two seats on the bus. Bravo Tim."

Cheryl nodded. "So you do see it."

Didi blew out air. "Whatever makes you happy." Didi clinked her glass against Cheryl's and they both chugged their wine down.

* * *

When I got home, Cheryl seemed excited to see me. I guess she forgave me for the bath thing. She had new glasses on and kissed me like there was a bull's-eye on my lips. Then she called me by a new nickname--Indiana. I kind of like it.

It was a disturbing experience working at ASD Accounting, but I guess I learned some things. It doesn't matter whether you work nine to five, five to nine, or whatever, your job may have issues. You just have to figure out how to deal with them. And maybe my relatives were wrong. Perhaps on occasion you do need to stand up and fight back.

The good news is that Cheryl and I got married this fall. It was wonderful. I decided to surprise her with a little musical interlude at the wedding. For some reason, her and Didi seemed terrified when I brought out my clarinet case. I think it was because they knew I hadn't played in public before. But they calmed right down when I removed my instrument and began serenading them with the new note I'd learned. I guess it's true what they say, music soothes the savage beast.

Oh, and by the way, I've started up my own hot dog truck business. But I'm going to run it right. I won't steal ideas and I'll promote employees if they deserve it. Most importantly, I will motivate them the old fashioned way--without bats, guns or roughing people up.

But you never know.

# In the Air Tonight
## Marilyn Todd

**CHLOE…**

… is sitting cross-legged on her sister's living room floor. Around her is what looks like bomb damage, but in reality is just the side-effect of planning the brightest, bestest, happiest wedding in the weddingverse. Fabric swatches for the bride. Fabric swatches for the bridesmaids. Fabric swatches for the flower girls, the page boys, in fact anyone and everyone who needs to be co-ordinated. And the reason that they're scattered is because no decisions have been made, which applies equally to the cake, the bouquets, the shoes, the something old, the something new, the something borrowed, something blue, the list goes on. None of which has any bearing on why Chloe is sitting cross-legged on Jessie's floor. It's just that she was the last to arrive, and all the other places had been nabbed.

After all, how can you possibly have the brightest, bestest, happiest wedding in the weddingverse if you don't have the brightest, bestest, happiest of send-offs?

'So where's it to be?' Jessie asked. 'Paris?'

The maid of honour wrinkled her nose. 'It always rains.'

'Venice?'

'Are you kidding?' The youngest bridesmaid rolled her eyes. 'The streets are flooded!'

'Rome, then?'

This hen party wasn't going to be confined to a night down the pub. This was destined for serious fun. You only had to watch the speed that the level was dropping in the tequila to see that.

'How about all three at the same time, with New York thrown in for good measure?' Chloe said.

Sixteen eyeballs bulged at once. 'You don't mean…?'

'I bloody do mean that.' Chloe punched the air. 'LAS VEGAS, BABY!'

Seriously. You could hear the squeals on Mars.

* * *

**JESS**…

…is lying face down on the bed, texting her fiancé from the room in the Luxor Pyramid that she shares with her sister. Given the eight-hour time difference between London and Nevada, conversation with Ryan was as limited as it was precious. Out of necessity, though, she'd had to brag about the Sphinx staring down outside the window. And while she was at it, boast about taking Paris, New York and Rome by storm, not forgetting the gondola on the Grand Canal—

'Which runs inside—yes, Ryan actually inside—the Venetian.'

How else was she supposed to watch him turn green with envy?

'You know my stag do is just one night in Blackpool?' Ryan laughed.

'Eat your heart out, loser,' Jessie giggled back.

At which point their precious "us" time would take a way more intimate turn, with videos that you wouldn't show your mother.

Which is why the full, unexpurgated details of the girls' exploits ended up consigned to text, and in the wee, small hours at that. After all, who in their right mind comes to Vegas to sleep? Time enough for that on the flight home, thank you very much.

So tap-tap-tap about pink flamingos, erupting volcanoes, model galleons floating in artificial coves, that half-size Eiffel Tower, the Trevi Fountain, and let's not forget the streets of Montmartre (indoors, naturally) where, when you sit in the chairs, it looks like you're wearing a lace up corset. Best of all, of course, was tilting out 1,000 feet above the Strip from the top of the Strat, where the only thing between you and the concrete below is your breakfast.

OK, not *all* unexpurgated commentary. Jess missed out the bit where sharing a room with Chloe was more theory than reality. That she'd hardly seen her sister once she'd got chatting to the bloke beside her on the plane. Talk about hitting it off, but so much for this girls-just-wanna-have-fun trip. Sure, Chloe was up for the Paris/Rome/Venice capers, but she'd baled for pretty much every shot, cocktail and thrill ride that the rest of them had been road-testing their nerves on.

Jack, it turned out, was embarking on a six-week contract overseeing the installation of some food processing plant on the outskirts of town. So yes, while he was at work, Chloe was very much an active hen—but once Jack clocked off, it was a different story. Quite frankly, Jessie didn't know whether to be excited to see Chloe so happy, or pissed that her sister kept bunking off.

'You're just jealous,' Chloe snapped, on one of the rare occasions that ships passed in the night. 'You're just jealous, because Jack's rich.'

'No, I'm not, and no, he isn't,' Jessie countered. 'His father won the lottery, not him, and how old did you say his dad is? Fifty-six?'

'Fifty-six next birthday, that's not the point. One day, Jack will inherit £9.7 million and you're jealous.'

'I'm going to take that insult with a pinch of salt, maybe some lime, but definitely tequila,' Life's too short to argue when the Fremont Street Experience beckons. 'You coming?'

'Nope. Jack and I are off to ride the roller coaster at New York, New York,' Chloe said, 'and look, I'm sorry I was such a bitch back there. You know me and my temper. I get carried away, I never mean what I said. The thing is, you and Ryan have something special going, it's me who's jealous, and besides.' She laughed. 'That ten mill is far from guaranteed. One false move, just one tiny indiscretion, he says, and his dad will cut him off without a penny.'

Jack's mum, it transpired, had been stabbed to death by some coke-head simply for not giving him the money in her purse.

'Poor cow didn't even get to see her fiftieth birthday.'

Jack's dad wasn't just devastated by the horror, loss and the senselessness of what happened, the shock brought on a heart attack.

'He's fine now, thanks to four stents, and determined to live life to the full. Even so, he swore that if he ever finds that Jack's taken anything stronger than an aspirin, he'll disinherit him.'

Because that was the tragedy. That cocaine-snorting drugged-up yob was her own son. Jack's brother. And for all that her husband won the lottery three years down the line, money doesn't buy you happiness at all, it really doesn't.

Jessie feels for them, but she's still not telling Ryan any of this. She's buggered if she'll see her little sister upstage this bloody wedding! Instead, Jess closes her eyes and pictures the beam of light shining straight up from the top of the Pyramid, so bright you can see it from space.

She sighs. Three days down, one still to go, and tons left on the list.

Bring it on!

* * *

**JACK** …

… cannot sleep. He doesn't understand why, when everything felt so right, it went so wrong.

Did he believe in love at first sight? No. Leastways, not for him. His parents always laughed about how that's what happened with them, but that's rare. Or rather was, until it seems he'd inherited the gene.

One glance at the girl beside him on the plane, and he was hooked. The more they chatted, the deeper he fell, and from then on, every second apart was sheer agony. Each touch was electric. She felt it, too. They shared every secret, bared both of their souls, a mutual vulnerability that brought them even closer. Yes, of course they'd just met, yes, of course they'd only known each other a few days, and yes of course there was so much to learn. But was it so daft, so very silly, to think about building a future together?

Which is why, on her last night in Vegas, as they stood beside the fountains dancing to Andrea Bocelli outside the Bellagio, Jack dropped down on one knee.

'The song says it's time to say goodbye. I say it's a good time to start a new life.' He whipped out an elastic band, the only thing he had on the spur of the moment. 'I'm handsome, I'm successful, I'm rich and I'm modest. So will you marry me, Chloe?'

He'd expected at least thirty seconds of indecision. It took five.

'You honestly think I'd marry someone for their money?' Anger blazed in those lovely blue eyes. 'You don't know me at all.'

And that was it. In the fraction of a second it took him to struggle to his feet in the pressing crowd, she was gone. Swallowed up by a million and one tourists, wiping their eyes to a song that suddenly rang horribly true.

It got worse. He realised then that he didn't know her last name, where she worked, where she lived. He knew every dark fear, every worst secret. But the basics?

Sod his contract. The next day was spent pacing the airport, checking out flights to the UK. He had no way of knowing if it was direct or connecting, or even what time, or whether he'd missed them completely. With an airport that size, especially with Vegas a magnet for hen parties, weddings and stag do's, one more group of girls could easily have got lost in the crush.

Unsurprisingly, the Luxor refused to divulge any information about their guests.

Obsessive internet searches and social media stalking came up empty, too. Nothing about upcoming nuptuals between any Ryans and Jessicas, which was no great shock. He remembered Chloe telling him, on the plane over, how Jess went by her middle name.

He obviously tried calling, texting, you name it, and got other people to do it for him, in case she'd blocked his number. Still nada, zilch and zip. It was a pay-as-you-go. Clearly, she'd paid and she'd gone.

Heartbroken, lonely and confused, Jack had no choice. He had a food processing plant to get up and running. Just man up and see this contract through, because, on the bright side, things couldn't get any worse.

No, wait.

Things did get worse.

Five weeks later, he was passing through airport security when a sniffer dog alerted its handler to Jack's carry-on.

'That's not mine!'

How many times had they heard that, he wondered dully.

'Let me get this straight. You have a bag of cocaine between the lining of your case and the shell, but someone slipped it in there by mistake, is that what you're saying?'

'No. I'm saying I don't know how it got there.'

However hard he insisted, however much he denied it, the truth was, the lining of his travel bag had been unzipped at some point, and a small bag of cocaine pushed inside. Invisible, undetectable—except by sniffer dogs.

Who? How? When? Where? The questions buzzed like a swarm of locusts, until it reached the point where Jack was simply glad he was done for possession not trafficking, and able to catch a flight home three days later.

'Meet you at the airport,' his dad had texted.

The relief, oh the relief. He could do with some good family bonding, knowing Dad wouldn't disinherit him over some idiot mistaking his carry-on for somebody else's. God, how they'd laugh it off over a beer, and there were no words, none, to describe seeing the beam on his father's face as he stood waving at Arrivals.

'Hey, son! Who said lightning couldn't strike twice?'

'Uh—Gimme a clue, Dad.'

'Love at first sight! Your mother and me! Well, guess what? It happened again, Jack. I got married.' If possible, the grin got even wider. 'Chloe, love, meet your new stepson.'

# Our Lips Are Sealed
## *Teresa Inge*

"Let's get this show on the road," Casey Everly yelled to Sadie Gentry, her sister and social media influencer, as she closed the door on her custom mobile bar camper.

"We have plenty of time. OBX is just an hour away." Sadie slipped into the passenger's seat next to Casey, now at the wheel of the black truck. The OBX was the local vernacular for the Outer Banks, a string of barrier islands off the east coast of North Carolina and a magnet for beach vacations and destination weddings.

"True, but you know how antsy the bride-to-be is that nothing goes wrong with the wedding shower." Casey pulled out of her driveway, hauling Silver Charm, a 1950 style caravan camper she'd converted into a vintage mobile bar and stocked with every libation possible.

"So, what's the plan?" Sadie asked.

Casey viewed her side mirror and changed lanes before crossing the North Carolina line. "When we get there, Earl Harper, the bride's brother and groomsman will meet us at his beach house to setup."

"Why isn't the bride meeting us?"

"She'll be along later with the bridal party, but he's hosting it for her."

"So, the usual setup?" Sadie asked.

"Yeah, but with an eighties vibe since the bride and groom were born in that decade."

"Last weekend it was Motown sixties music, and the week before songs of the seventies, and before that hip-hop and pop. I think we've covered all the eras." Sadie laughed.

"And then some," Casey said. "That's what we do. We create vintage mobile bar events for our guests to enjoy and we do it well."

Just three years apart, the sisters, attractive and fit, were best friends, and could handle most situations that came their way while hosting events. They chatted and spent the ride over the Wright Memorial bridge singing their favorite hits. When the first notes of "Our Lips are Sealed" played, Casey squealed and cranked up the volume. The pair sang loudly until they reached the outskirts of Kill Devil Hills. A quiet little town on the thin strip of the barrier island.

"There's Durham Street." Sadie pointed toward the beach side of the bypass where the wedding shower was taking place. Casey pulled into the driveway of the three-story house with an ocean view.

A man dressed in white shorts, flip flops, and a long-sleeved polo shirt trotted down the front steps of the house with a koozie in his hand. The rubber holder did not completely cover the label of a popular beer brand. He walked toward the truck. "Park the camper in the grass to the right of the house. You can setup there."

Casey leaned her head out of the window. "Is there an electrical supply nearby?"

"It's near the fence. I'll show you after you park."

She eased the camper onto the grass.

"He's a handsome devil," Sadie said, sneaking a sideways peek.

"If you like preppy, pink-shirted guys," Casey joked.

After they parked, the man approached the sisters, eyeing them up and down as they exited the vehicle. Ignoring his rude behavior, Casey faced him. "I'm Casey, owner of Casey's Vintage Mobile Bar Events."

"You're also late," he took a long swig of beer.

She viewed the time on her phone. Eleven-forty-five. She was fifteen minutes early, and it was way too soon for him to be chugging beer.

"And you are?" Casey gave the man a side eye as she unhooked the camper.

"Earl Harper, Belinda's brother. You know, the bride-to-be," he said, giving her a smug look. "Do you have the setup instructions she sent you?"

"Uh…yeah." Casey scanned the area. "Where's the electrical supply?"

"You mean besides me?" Earl chuckled.

She held the power cord up in her hand and tried not to roll her eyes.

"Oh…you mean a plug in? This way."

The sisters followed him toward a metal box by the fence some thirty feet from the truck. Casey plugged the mobile bar cord into the outlet while Sadie opened the concession window. "Do you have the wedding supplies? Belinda said they would be here," she asked Earl.

"They're in a large black storage container on the front porch. It's marked wedding items. You can't miss it."

Casey and Sadie grabbed the heavy container from the porch with no help from Earl. They dug through the items.

"We've got bridal plates, cups, utensils, and eighties decorations." Sadie held up neon cutouts of cassette players, boom boxes, Cabbage Patch dolls, and Pac-Man.

"Gag me with a spoon. It's 1989 again." Casey placed her hands on her hips and scanned the area. "Let's set up the tents over there and then we'll add the doodads from the Decade of Excess."

An hour later, the setup took shape as the women placed tables and chairs under the tents. "Grab the cutlery and koozies and put them on the food table but leave room for the food trays," Casey instructed her sister. "I'll add the decorations and lights around the tents and mobile bar."

Casey grabbed two baskets of white roses and hung one on each end of the retro camper. The camper had as much appeal to guests as the event itself.

She placed a stand-up chalkboard in front of the serving window that listed specialty cocktails, beer, and wine options for guests.

Dusting her hands on her pants, Casey let out a puff of air that fluttered her hair.

"Totally eighties," Sadie said with a shake of her head.

"I want my MTV." Casey laughed as a white SUV pulled into the driveway. The door opened and a pair of white flip flops attached to Belinda's tanned legs slid out of the vehicle. Two striking blonde sisters, Jane and Gina Hart followed suit. Belinda made her way toward Casey and Sadie. The blondes dogged her heels.

"Who brought these hideous decorations?" Belinda yelled.

"Uh…Earl gave them to us to set up," Casey said.

Before Belinda could respond, Earl appeared. "Hey Sis. Do you like the decorations?"

"They're tacky," she frowned.

"What do you girls think?" Earl asked the two bridesmaids who stood next to Belinda with their arms crossed in a defiant stance. "It's awful," Jane said.

"I want to gag." Gina pointed her index finger into her mouth.

Not wanting to take sides between the siblings, Casey cleared her throat. "I have other decorations in the truck that you might like better."

"I don't know why I ever listened to my knucklehead brother," Belinda said. She turned toward Casey. "I have to get ready for the shower. Fix these god-awful decorations." She grabbed her bags from the vehicle and stormed off to the house with the blondes in tow.

Casey and Sadie stood dumbstruck.

"You heard her. Fix it!" Earl headed to the porch.

"Oh-mi-god. Bridezilla and her brother." Casey's eyebrows knitted together. The sisters grabbed the items from the truck and blended them with the decorations.

Thirty minutes later, Belinda raced down the outdoor stairs in a white robe marked Bride. "At least there's a coastal vibe now with the decorations."

Casey exhaled. After Belinda went back to the house, she and Sadie made pre-made batches of cocktails and tested the beer tap.

"I'll grab the coolers and fill them with ice," Sadie said as Casey placed the batches in the refrigerator.

Moments later, a BBQ truck pulled into the driveway. Earl instructed the two large men in the truck to place the serving trays on the food tables. He said to Casey, "They'll be back later to pick up the trays and haul away all trash from the event."

Casey arranged the trays after reminding Sadie not to throw them away after the event. They finished their setup in comfortable silence.

Earl approached the sisters. "It's three o'clock. Guests will arrive soon. Make sure you're ready," he smirked.

*Oh, brother.* Casey stepped inside the camper's tiny kitchen. She had purchased the vehicle for a song and restored it with a refrigerator, sink, beer tap, and shelves. A local body shop painted it silver for its retro appeal. After raising her family, divorcing her cheating husband, and retiring from the food and beverage industry, Casey's investment in the mobile bar allowed her to be her own boss.

Sadie grabbed her phone and snapped photos of the setup, food, and beach house. "Come on Sis, let's take our obligatory photo." Casey stepped in front of the camera flashing a bright smile. The women sported white t-shirts with Casey's Vintage Mobile Bar Events.

"I'll post these to social media and our website and take more photos during the event," Sadie offered. As a social media fashion influencer and former model, she handled the marketing for her older sister's business.

"Great, especially since the photos get us more jobs," Casey smiled.

"Thanks to our followers who share them."

Moments later, Belinda and her blonde entourage emerged from the beach house, all wearing white shorts and pink t-shirts. Belinda's shirt sported "Bride," and the blondes, "Bridesmaids."

"Uh-oh. The blonde ambition is headed our way," Sadie mumbled as they approached the bar.

"The mobile bar is A-dorable," Jane said.

"Selfie time!" Gina squealed.

"Give us the Orange Crush." Belinda gestured toward the chalkboard options.

To the right of the bar, a DJ who had arrived earlier sound-checked his equipment. As Casey and Sadie poured drinks from the pre-made batch, the bridal party snapped more selfies by the camper. Other guests lined up to order cocktails and take photos which kept the sisters busy for the next hour.

Jane appeared at the serving window. "My Orange Crush is sour."

Casey viewed an empty glass in the woman's hand and realized this was her fourth visit to the window. "I'm sorry that happened. Would you like a bottled water instead?"

"No. Just give me a glass of white wine."

Casey held her temper. "You've had enough already. I cannot serve you anymore alcohol at this time."

"I would think you would serve better drinks for the price that Belinda paid you," her voice angry and slurred.

"Again, I'm sorry that happened."

Jane slammed her glass against the serving shelf and stormed off.

Sadie approach Casey. "You okay?"

"Yeah." Casey grabbed the shatterproof glass and wiped down the shelf with a bar towel.

"Well, it's not the first time you've cut someone off nor will it be the last."

Shrugging off the incident, the sisters served drinks as the DJ played eighties music and guests mingled.

Earl approached the mobile bar. "I need the champagne that Belinda requested for the toast." His face was red and twisted but his speech appeared normal.

Casey realized Earl was sunburnt from the blazing sun. "Just a moment." She grabbed the bottle from one of the coolers but hesitated, assessing his intoxication before handing it to him. "Do you need sunscreen?"

"Just give me the bottle. It's hot out here," he extended his hand toward her.

Moments later the DJ spoke into a microphone, "Good afternoon everyone. Please gather by the tent to toast the bride and groom."

Belinda and groom, Jax Taylor, stood under the tent as guests approached them. Casey placed a back in fifteen minutes sign on the bar's shelf and stepped out of the camper with Sadie to hear the toast.

"Be right back. I have to go to the restroom," Casey said.

"Most of you know that the bride and groom have been friends since grade school. But what brought them together as teenagers is their love for each other and eighties music. So, let's raise a glass to the couple and wish them a lifetime of happiness and all things eighties," the DJ said.

"Hear, hear," a woman raised her glass.

As the bride and groom sipped champagne, members of the bridal party gave speeches. Gina grabbed the microphone. "My sister and I have known Belinda and Jax since the first grade. We knew they were perfect for each other when they held their wedding ceremony in our backyard in third grade."

"Whoo-hoo," a man shouted.

The DJ called for Earl to toast the couple. The crowd glanced around the area. He called Earl's name again with no response. A scream resounded from the mobile bar. Casey and Sadie ran toward it. A woman stood by the camper's door, near a female body lying on the ground by the bloody coolers. Blood dripped on her collar and the grass from a gash in the head.

A small crowd gathered nearby.

"Excuse me. I'm a doctor." A female made her way through the crowd. She knelt and pushed back the long blonde hair. She shook her head.

* * *

After the medical examiner left with the body, the police identified the victim as Jane Hart, a bridesmaid in Belinda's wedding.

Moments later, Earl stumbled down the beach house stairs. Casey, Sadie, and Belinda stood by Gina as she wiped tears from her eyes.

"Where have you been?" Belinda asked her brother.

He rubbed his eyes. "Passed out in the upstairs bedroom. The heat got to me."

"So, you don't know what happened?"

He had a puzzled look.

"Jane was found dead by the mobile bar."

Before Earl could respond, a man in a blue shirt and navy pants approached the group. "I'm Detective Eric Ryan. I'd like to ask you a few questions about Jane Hart," he said to Casey.

"Me?" Casey touched her chest.

"Yes. I understand that you and Jane argued earlier. Can you tell me what happened?”

Casey frowned. “She was upset that I cut her off.”

“Can you elaborate?”

Casey spent the next ten minutes describing her business and Jane’s condition that led to the alcohol ban.

“Then what happened?”

“She smashed the glass onto the serving shelf and stormed off.”

“Where did she go?”

“I don’t know. I got busy serving drinks and never her saw again.”

“What did Ms. Hart drink from your bar?”

Sadie interrupted. “Orange Crush.”

“And you are?”

“Sadie Gentry, Casey’s sister.”

The detective pulled a small note pad and pen from his shirt pocket. He jotted down a few notes. “Since Ms. Hart said her drink was sour, did other guests complain as well?”

The sisters shook their heads.

The detective turned and faced Casey. “Where is the glass that Ms. Hart used?”

“In the trash under the sink.”

“Do you have the pre-made batch that she drank from?”

“There’s a small amount left in the refrigerator,” Casey said. “But no one else complained of it tasting sour.”

Gina stepped toward Casey. Belinda and Earl stood behind her. “You killed my sister,” she blurted.

“Look. I know everyone is upset but I need you all to step away from the camper while my team and I conduct our investigation.” Detective Ryan waved his hand toward Casey.

Casey’s legs shook. Does he think she poisoned her? Was he going to arrest her?

* * *

Three days later, Casey and Sadie remained holed up in their hotel room in OBX. With the mobile bar and truck confiscated and the beach house off limits for the investigation, the detective suggested the sisters not leave town until further notice and recommended they not post to social media.

"This is a fine fix we're in." Sadie laid on the bed scrolling through her photos. "I'm going stir crazy. Plus, I can't even post the event photos that I took to social media."

Casey rubbed her aching head after another restless night's sleep. She opened the balcony door to feel the salty air on her face.

"Who do you think did it? Murdered her, I mean," Sadie asked.

"The police didn't say she was murdered."

"But all signs are pointing that way otherwise they wouldn't have told us to stay here. And how did she get that gash on her head?"

"I don't know."

Three quick knocks appeared on the door. Casey opened it.

Detective Ryan stood in the hallway. "May I come in?"

Casey widened the door and stood back.

"I have additional questions," he said.

"Have a seat." She pointed toward the desk chair and sat next to Sadie on the bed.

"First, I appreciate you staying in OBX the past few days. I know it's been stressful."

"Three of my clients canceled their events due to the news reporting my business is related to Jane's death," Casey said.

"Unfortunately, news and social media outlets have their own agenda." The detective pulled a paper from his pocket. "I received the forensic report. Jane died from head trauma. Her blood alcohol level was twice the legal limit."

"What does that mean?" Casey asked.

"She either fell or was hit with a blunt object. And she was really drunk."

"So, the ingredients in the Orange Crush were okay?"

"Yes."

"Where did it happen?" Sadie asked.

"That I don't know. But from the house security footage, after Jane slammed the glass at the mobile bar, she mingled a while then headed inside the beach house. A short while later Casey entered the house. Which bears the question, why were you in the house?" he asked.

"I used the bathroom," Casey said.

"What didn't you use the portable outside?"

"I wanted to freshen up…and I hate portable johns."

"Did you see Jane while you were in the house?"

"Uh…no. I went to the bathroom, then returned to the toasting ceremony. Is there video of Jane leaving the house?"

"Only up to the time you entered. The rest of the footage is unclear."

"How did blood get on the coolers?" Casey asked.

"She possibly collapsed against them before hitting the ground." He paused. "I have one last question…"

Casey's eyes widened.

"Did you kill her?"

Fear swept Casey's body. She trembled to get the words out of her mouth. She took a deep breath. "No."

* * *

The police released her property and told her they would be in touch. After retrieving her camper, Casey worried she was still a suspect as she drove to Earl's beach house. She and Sadie placed the tents, tables, and other supplies into the truck bed.

"What do you want to do with the eighties decorations?" Sadie wiped down the coolers.

"I'm glad someone packed the decorations in the storage container for us. Let's put them on the front porch where we found them." Casey walked toward the container to make sure the lid was closed tight.

"Some party." Sadie loaded the oversized coolers into the back of the truck.

"You can say that again." Casey glanced at the eerily quiet beach house. "The house feels spooky."

"I hope Detective Ryan figures out what happened to Jane," Sadie said.

"What I don't understand is that no one at the party saw what happened to her. Plus, that's the only reason the detective is letting us leave town, since he can't prove that she was murdered without video, photos, or a witness. Right now, they're classifying it as accidental." Casey shook her head.

Sadie had a puzzled expression.

"What's wrong?" Casey asked.

Sadie scrolled through photos on her phone that she took during the shower. She pressed her thumb and index finger together to enlarge a photo and turned the camera toward Casey.

Casey's mouth flew open. "Why didn't you mention this sooner?"

"I didn't think anything of it until now that we're talking about photos. I remembered that when you went in the house to use the bathroom, a cute couple took photos in front of the mobile bar and the house. I asked if I could snap a few shots of them for our social media."

"And…"

"That's when I realized in the background behind the couple that Earl had his arm around Jane as they entered the house together."

"How could you forget that?"

Sadie shrugged. "Since I didn't know anyone at the event, I wasn't aware of who was dating whom. Do you think it's related to Jane's death?"

"I don't know. I just want to get the heck out of here." Casey pressed the lid down on the bin that kept protruding open. "Help me lift this to the front porch," she asked her sister.

"It's heavier than before. Belinda must have shoved other items into it."

The front door of the house opened. "How's it going?" Gina stepped down the stairs and approached the sisters with tape in her hand.

They set the bin on the ground. "We're finishing up," Casey said.

"We didn't realize anyone was here," Sadie added.

"I came by to see Earl."

"Oh. How is Earl?" Casey asked.

"Better now."

"I remember he was sunburnt pretty bad."

"You can leave the bin where it is," Gina said.

"We were putting it back on the porch where Earl had it."

"Not necessary. The BBQ people will be by shortly to pick up their trays and any extra trash we have. The decorations are being throw away with the rest of it."

"Uh…okay." Just as the women turned to leave, the container lid popped opened. "I can't get this to stay shut." Casey pulled the lid off the bin to straighten out whatever kept causing the issue.

"Oh-mi-God!" Sadie put her hand over her mouth.

Casey's eyes widened. "It's…it's…Earl."

Gina moved closer and pushed the body way down into the container and covered it with decorations. She placed the lid on it and taped it shut tightly.

"What happened to him?" Casey asked.

"I killed him after I found out he killed Jane."

"But why?"

"Earl and Jane had a thing going. Jane found out she was pregnant, but he denied it was his. They argued, and he struck her in the head. She stumbled outside and collapsed by your camper." Gina wiped tears from her eyes.

"But how do you know that when there were no witnesses?" Casey asked.

"Let's just say that I used my charm and persuasion to find that out from Earl before he died."

"The police will figure it out," Sadie said.

"Not if you don't tell them. Especially, since my version will be that I caught you two shoving Earl's body into your cooler and the back of your truck after you killed him."

"How could you do that?" Sadie asked.

"Look. You two are sisters. You would protect each other too," Gina said.

"But this isn't protecting your sister. Let the police handle it," Casey pleaded.

The BBQ truck pulled into the driveway. The two men got out and grabbed the food trays, trash, and eighties decorations.

Casey eyed Sadie then Gina. "Our lips are sealed."

# The Safety Dance
## Michael Bracken

"We can dance if we want to!" Maria insisted after a white-haired older man the size, shape, and demeanor of an antique upright freezer had stopped the music by stomping on their boom box and kicking over the tie-died bucket hat in which they'd been collecting change from passersby.

The human freezer pointed at the *No Loitering* sign posted on the parking garage wall behind Maria before folding his thick arms across his thicker chest and glaring icily at her.

As Willie retrieved the change scattered across the sidewalk and returned it to the hat, Sally took Maria's arm and tugged. "Let's just go."

Maria resisted her friend's forceful urging and stretched up on her tiptoes to stare into the iceman's cold blue eyes. "I'll bet you can't dance, and if you can't dance, you're no friend of mine!"

He blinked but said nothing.

By then, Willie had collected all the change and had tucked the broken boom box under his arm. "Let's go, Maria."

Reluctantly, Maria let Sally pull her away from the street corner where they'd been dancing all morning, and she followed her two friends several blocks away, to a diner they had seen earlier that featured a blue-plate lunch special they could split three ways.

They attracted attention as they danced through the mid-day crowd of men and women in drab business suits and hair that had been lacquered into helmets. With free-flowing locks that hung to mid-back, the two young women wore gauzy, multi-colored dresses that swirled around them as they moved, while Willie wore a blousy white shirt and form-fitting black ballet tights. Willie had transferred their morning take into his pockets and wore the bucket hat, while Sally wore a black top hat adorned with a peacock feather and Marie wore a red beret. They all wore scuffed black jazz dance shoes.

Later, as they divided the plate-sized chicken-fried steak into three portions, Maria pointed to the boom box and asked Willie, "Can you fix it?"

He shook his head. "I don't think so."

"Do we have enough to buy a new one?"

He shook his head again.

They stared morosely at their lunch, interrupted in their despair when the waitress, a rail-thin woman whose wrinkled face was a roadmap of experience, limped over, placed a plate of lemon wedges on the table, and refilled their water glasses.

Sally looked up. "We didn't ask for lemons."

The woman smiled. She wore a pink and white uniform under a white waist apron and had a name plate over her right breast that read *Norma*. "Squeeze them into your water, child, add some sweetener, and you have poor man's lemonade."

"But we—"

"Don't try to fool me," the waitress said. "I know that look. I've seen it in the mirror more times than I can count."

They thanked her, made lemonade, and finished their lunch.

When Norma returned to clear away their empty plate and leave their check, she pointed to the damaged boombox. "What happened to that?"

Maria told her.

"You're dancers?" After they nodded, she drew back the check and stuffed it into one of her apron pockets. "I was once. Two years with the Radio City Rockettes."

Sally asked. "What happened?"

"I tried to dance with a taxi," she said. "My leg hasn't been the same since."

After Norma limped away, Willie said, "Puts things in perspective, doesn't it?"

They left a fistful of change on the table, collected their things, and headed home to the one-room third-floor walk-up they shared. Except for a small bathroom with a toilet, shower, and sink, the one room served as living room, kitchen, bedroom, and dance studio.

Knowing they would have to wear their outfits several more times before they would be laundered, the roommates hung their dance clothes on the shower curtain and spritzed them with cheap perfume.

Willie dumped the remaining change from that morning onto their tiny table and counted the two crumpled singles and pile of coins. After adding what they had to what they had left for Norma, Willie told the others what they had earned. "Definitely more than we've ever earned on a weekday morning."

"Then we need to go back there," Maria said.

"Not if we have to deal with the creep who ran us off," Sally said.

"And buy a new boombox every time he does," Willie added.

*  *  *

Opportunities were sparse during the next several weeks. Willie auditioned to play a sapling in a traveling children's theatre troupe but lost the role to a guy who was taller and thinner, Sally turned down the opportunity to pop out of a cake and dance topless for a bachelor's party, and Maria applied for a job teaching country line dancing at a popular bar but didn't get the position because she didn't own cowboy boots.

As always, the dancing roommates worked temp jobs, taking whatever soul-crushing assignments came their way. Sally spent two weeks in a corporation's mailroom. Willie picked up three days unloading trucks and several more picking goods in a warehouse. Maria, who could type, worked a series of office jobs. Together, they scraped together enough to pay the rent, put food on the table, and purchase a used boombox from the pawn shop down the block from their apartment building. They practiced a few new dance moves, careful not to knock over their only lamp, and planned to return to the park that weekend.

Maria hadn't been able to stop thinking about the waitress who had been kind enough to buy their lunch. So, Friday evening, she was standing outside the diner when Norma clocked out. The young dancer wore a loose-fitting, short-sleeve gray T-shirt over faded blue jeans and running shoes, her black hair pulled back into a loose ponytail under the tie-dye bucket hat usually used to collect change.

Maria stopped the older woman. "Can I ask you a question?"

Despite the change in Maria's attire, Norma recognized her. "Walk with me, child, you can ask all the questions you want."

Maria matched her pace to Norma's slow but steady limp. "After the accident, did you stop dancing?"

"Not being able to dance professionally hurt worse than the accident, but I never stopped dancing. I just stopped dancing on stage and started dancing for my cat." She did a stutter step and a slow spin.

Maria smiled. "Do you work tomorrow morning?"

"No, but—"

"Then come dance with us."

"You don't want some old woman—"

"Tomorrow morning," Maria insisted. She told Norma that she and her friends would be at the park and told her when they planned to arrive.

Norma stopped in front of a brownstone. "This is me."

"Tomorrow," Maria said. "You won't forget?"

"No, child, I won't forget."

* * *

The next morning, Maria, Sally, and Willie set up in the center of the park, next to the fountain. Sally put out the tie-dyed bucket hat and Willie turned on the boombox. And they danced. They danced together and separately. They were joyous in their movements, their skirts and shirts and hair flowing about them and catching the attention of passersby. Little children danced with them or stared googly-eyed from a distance as parents held them back.

Maria kept watch for her invited guest, but Norma had not arrived by the time they took a break for lunch. The grizzled man at the hot dog cart, who had been watching all morning, gave them chili dogs and bottles of water.

"You make an old man smile," he said. "So free! So graceful!"

They sat on the edge of the fountain basin and ate their lunch, Maria still watching for her guest.

"She's not coming," Sally said.

"She promised."

"Wouldn't be the first time someone broke a promise," Willie said. "Remember the time—"

"That was different," Maria insisted, even though she wasn't certain which broken promise Willie was referring to.

They danced for two hours after lunch. By then they were tired and hot and were seeing diminishing returns for their efforts. They gathered their things and walked home from the park. Willie stopped at a grocery store, while the other two continued on. When they reached their building, Maria told Sally she wanted to see why Norma hadn't joined them.

"Be back by dinnertime?" Sally asked.

"What are we having?"

"Pasta. Willie's picking up spaghetti and a jar of Prego and a pound of hamburger."

Maria smiled. "I'll be back."

She made her way to Norma's brownstone and examined all the mailboxes. She didn't know Norma's last name, but she did find N. Braun in apartment 2B. She leaned into the bell and waited. After a minute, she heard, "Hello?"

"Norma, it's Maria."

"I don't know any Marias."

"The dancer. You were supposed to join us in the park this

morning."

Silence stretched out for so long Maria thought Norma had forgotten about her. Then the door buzzer sounded. Maria let herself in and hurried up the stairs. Norma was waiting with her apartment door open.

"Are you okay?" Maria asked as she rushed past Norma and into her living room. "I was worried about you."

Maria stopped, wide-eyed. A black cat sat on a credenza below a yellowing poster promoting the Radio City Rockettes. She walked up to the poster and examined it. She looked at Norma and then back at the poster, finally pointing at the dancer second from the left. "That's you, isn't it?"

"That's me, child, two weeks before I became a taxi dancer."

"A taxi dancer? You weren't—" And then Maria grasped the joke. "I'm sorry."

"You weren't driving the taxi, so there's nothing you need be sorry for."

"I know, but—"

"I was about to make tea," Norma said. "And I have some shortbread cookies."

After Norma disappeared into the kitchen, Maria examined all the autographed photographs hanging on the walls, a who's who of dancers from back in the day. When Norma returned with two cups of tea and a box of shortbread cookies tucked under her arm, Maria asked, "You knew all these people?"

"I danced with most of them. I was in the chorus usually, but—"

"But still." Maria took one of the cups from Norma, and they settled into a pair of wingback chairs older than break dancing. The black cat jumped into Maria's lap and settled into place.

"Many of them are gone now," Norma said.

"But you're not.

"No, child, I'm not."

"So, tell me what it was like."

For the next several hours, Norma described it all. The stage. The lights. The music. The audience. The other dancers. She regaled the younger dancer with stories about the past, about the dance lessons, the auditions, and the tiny parts in major productions. She told her about her big break when she joined the Rockettes. "It was everything I ever dreamed of, until—"

Maria reached for a cookie. "Until?"

"I'll never forget that night," Norma said. "We'd just finished our Sunday show, and I was headed home. I stepped off the curb just as a taxi came barreling around the corner. The driver didn't see me in time. He stood on the brakes, but, well—" She motioned toward her leg. "He left me with this. I'll never forget him, either. He got out of the cab, looked at me, and then got back in and drove away."

"A hit-and-run."

Norma nodded. "Luckily, one of the other dancers wrote down the taxi number and reported him. The driver—Ivan Davidson—lost his license, paid a fine, and was sentenced to a significant amount of community service. The judge had a unique way of balancing justice's scale. She assigned him to a community center with a significant dance program for local children. Though he cut short one dancer's career, he help dozens of young dancers get their start."

Marie finished her cookie, downed the last of her tea, and asked, "Why didn't you join us at the park?"

Norma looked away for a moment, then returned her attention to Maria. "It was kind of you to ask, and I considered joining you—I really did—but I don't dance for anyone but Bob Fosse."

At the sound of his name, the cat lifted his head and meowed.

"Next time? Will you join us next time? Even if you don't dance you can share your stories with Sally and Willie. I know they'd love to hear them."

Norma said something non-committal, took Bob Fosse from Maria's lap, and saw the young woman to the door.

* * *

Over dinner, Maria, Sally, and Willie discussed their day at the park.

"It was barely worth our time," Willie said.

None of them had auditions or temp work on Wednesday, so they planned their next public performance. Sally and Willie made suggestions for a location, but Maria said, "You know where we need to go."

"No," Willie said. "We aren't going back there."

"We made more money there than anywhere else we've performed on a weekday."

"And had to use it to buy a new boombox."

They argued until the other two finally caved to Maria.

Tuesday evening, on her way home from a one-day temp job as a receptionist for a law firm, Maria stopped at the diner, caught Norma's attention, and told her where they would be performing the next morning.

"Thank you, but I have to work, child," Norma said. "Bob Fosse needs his kibble."

* * *

Wednesday morning, Maria, Sally, and Willie set up their boombox and collection hat and began dancing beneath the *No Loitering* sign on the parking garage wall for all the office workers scurrying by. They had been dancing for an hour when the antique human freezer approached.

Willie grabbed the boombox. Sally grabbed the bucket hat. Maria kept dancing.

Their glacial-headed nemesis stopped in front of Maria. "I told you, no dancing."

Maria smiled and danced around him.

He pointed to the *No Loitering* sign. "I will call the police."

"You're rude."

"And you are an imbecile."

He reached for her arm, and she sidestepped him. Keeping time to the music, Maria moved to the left and moved to the right. He moved with her.

She danced to the light pole, to the pole holding the *No Parking* sign, and then back.

"See," she said, "you can dance."

"I'm not dancing."

He grabbed for her, this time wrapping his hand around her wrist.

She smiled up at him. His eyes were still ice blue. "You think you're ready to lead now? Do you have the rhythm? It's a waltz. It's one-two-three, one-two-three, one-two-three—"

People had stopped scurrying about and had stopped to watch what was happening.

"No. Stop. Stop dancing," he insisted. "Stop dancing now!"

"Let go of her!"

Maria turned to see Norma hurrying toward them, her limp more pronounced the faster she moved. Having come directly from the diner, he wore her pink and white uniform and white waist apron.

The human freezer's eyes widened as if he had seen a ghost. He released his hold on Maria and stepped backward until he was against the garage wall beneath the *No Loitering* sign.

"You!" Norma poked her forefinger into his chest. "What are you doing to these children?"

"No dancing," he insisted. "I had enough of dancing and dancers to last a lifetime."

Willie turned off the boombox. Without music, the sounds of the city returned.

"You want to kill their dreams like you killed mine?"

Softly, he said, "That night killed my dreams, too."

Without the music and without the shouting, the activity at the corner became less interesting for the gathered crowd, and the audience drifted away until only the three dancers, Norma, and the man she had backed up against the wall remained. Maria looked from Ivan Davidson to Norma and back, watching Ivan's icy stare thaw and Norma's anger dissipate.

"Your dreams," Norma asked. "What dreams?"

He told her about losing his license, losing his job, and having to drop out of night school to serve his community service time. "I never went back. I never graduated. I never—"

He never finished whatever it was he wanted to say because Norma said, "All your life you've been living with this."

"All your life and mine," he said.

Norma turned to Willie. "Turn the music on. Give us a slow song."

Willie did as instructed.

Norma took Ivan's hand and urged him away from the wall. "You can dance. You know you can. Let the music move you. It will take us out of this world, and we can leave everything behind."

Maria and Sally and Willie watched the memories of what had derailed their lives slowly seep from Norma and Ivan as they became lost in the music.

The young dancers joined them, the passersby dropped money in the tie-dyed bucket hat, and everything worked out right.

# *Uptown Girl*
## *John M. Floyd*

J. Edwin Murphy leaned forward in the new chair in his new office and pushed the button on his new intercom. "Jennifer? I can't seem to get an outside line."

"Nobody can, yet," she said. "They'll connect us sometime this morning." Which wasn't surprising—this was the first day in their new downtown location, and everyone was still getting settled. Murphy had heard that his was the only office that already had its desk and gadgets and other furniture in place. That, too, made sense: he was the boss. That thought made him smile a bit. In the words of the great Mel Brooks, it's good to be da king.

His home life was another matter. Murphy had a younger wife, and, as she often reminded him, had married above his station in life. He had, however, been lucky in business if not lucky in love, and in the years since their wedding, his investment firm had grown and thrived like the overflowing kudzu in the woods around his hometown in the now-distant South. He supposed that that alone, and the fact that he still loved her, should've been enough for him. But it wasn't. He'd long ago realized he wouldn't be satisfied with the success he'd achieved until Annamarie (one word, not two—how was *that* for fancy-pantsy?) recognized his worth and his value. Even if she did, though, he doubted she would admit it.

King or not, it seemed that today he would have to climb down from his throne and use his cell phone, which he hated. With a sigh he put on his reading glasses, dug out his phone (an overrated toy, in his opinion), and studied the screen. At last he found the button that actually showed him a telephone keypad, and punched in the numbers.

After a long wait, an unfamiliar female voice answered. "Larrimore Investigations."

"Hello," Murphy said, frowning. "May I speak to Tom?"

"He's not in. My name's Madeira. I'm a colleague of Mr. Larrimore."

"Well, I'm a *client* of Mr. Larrimore, as of yesterday. He's supposed to do a job for me."

"Oh, my goodness. You're Mr. Murphy? I'm afraid Tom's out sick, sir. Meanwhile, he told me to step in."

Murphy paused, thinking that over. "How far in, exactly, have you stepped?"

"Well, I'm in a car right now, parked near your house. Two-five-four Stanford Street."

"So he told you what I need done?"

"Surveillance of your home," she said.

"Yes. All day, if necessary. Madeline, is it?"

"Madeira. It's an island my father once visited, near Portugal."

"Nice place, I hope."

"Daddy said it's beautiful."

"Well, Madeira, I need you to—"

"Tom calls me Maddy."

"—to watch the house and make note of any comings or goings."

"By anyone in particular?"

"By anyone at all. But especially visitors."

"Will your wife be out and about, do you think?"

"Not anytime soon." Murphy checked his watch. Nine a.m. Annamarie hadn't been out and about before noon since she graduated from high school. "You have a camera?" he asked.

"A phone camera, and a perfect angle to the house, from here."

"Good." As planned, this was Violet's day off. Violet was their housekeeper, a necessary evil because Annamarie couldn't cook a lick, and probably wouldn't even know how to turn the washing machine or vacuum cleaner on. Murphy was surprised he hadn't been asked to hire a butler. "Just stay out of sight," he said, "snap some photos, take notes."

"Understood."

"Great. Let me know if anyth—"

"Hang on."

Murphy frowned. "What?"

"I said 'hang on.' Somebody's coming."

He leaned back in his chair, waiting. A silence passed.

"False alarm," she said. "Jogger."

"Okay. Keep me informed." He disconnected and heaved another sigh. Outside his office, Murphy could hear voices, and the thumping and scraping of furniture and equipment being moved about. Either that, or a bumper-car race.

Twenty minutes later his cell phone buzzed. He jumped as if poked by a cattle prod.

"Mr. Murphy? A man just walked up, knocked on your front door, and went inside."

"Whoa," he said. So his suspicions were correct. "You took photos, I assume?"

"Yes—for what they're worth. The guy wore a baseball cap pulled low and a shirt collar pulled high, and kept his head down. Only thing I saw was a short, stocky dude in dark clothes."

"License plate number?"

"No car. He's on foot."

Murphy said nothing, taking this in.

"What should I do?" Maddy asked.

"What do you mean? What more *can* you do?"

After a pause, she said, "This visitor and your wife just walked past two unshaded windows toward the back of your house. I think they're on the back porch."

"Deck," he said. "But you still won't be able to see them. The back yard's fenced." As if she hadn't noticed that herself.

"I'm not talking about peeking through a fence. Your wife might not be out and about, but she's up and about. I saw her raise a window in a front room, earlier. Maybe as a signal."

"And?"

"And she didn't close it all the way."

Murphy felt himself frown. "You're not thinking about—"

"I'm small and I'm fast, Mr. Murphy. And quiet. I can go through the window, sneak to the back, take pictures of the two of them, and get out again."

He shook his head as if she could see him. "Bad idea. You get caught, you're in trouble." *And when Tom tells them I hired you, I'm in trouble.*

"I'm also very careful," she said. Murphy heard her open her car door. "Don't call me in the next few minutes, for obvious reasons. I'll phone you when I'm done."

Before he could say more, she disconnected. He sat there holding the phone to his ear awhile longer, then set it on his desk and stared at it. Why did bad decisions always seem to grow worse as time passed?

Six minutes later the phone buzzed. Holding his breath, he picked up.

"I'm in," Maddy said, her voice barely a whisper. "Back room, looking at 'em through a window to the deck. I'm taking pictures when I can see clear faces."

"What do you mean, 'when'?"

"They're both sort of…relaxing."

"They're what?"

"They're in the hot tub."

Murphy paused, drew a deep breath. He realized he was squeezing the phone so hard his fingers hurt. "You're certain? You saw them there?"

"Oh yes. I *see* them there."

At that point Murphy had another, even worse, thought. "Wait a second," he said. "This visitor—how *well* can you see him?"

"Pretty well." Then, after a pause: "Sometimes more'n I want to see."

"My point is"—she'd already said he was short and stocky—"is he middle-aged, fifty or so, black hair, going bald in front?"

"Yes. You know him?"

Silence. Murphy could almost feel his blood pressure spiking.

"Listen to me, Maddy," he said. "The man you're watching is named Anthony Perronti. He's wanted by the authorities." Another long, deep breath. "He and my wife had a…relationship…before she and I were married. Do you understand?"

"Not exactly."

What Maddy would *certainly* not understand, because Murphy didn't plan to tell her, was that Tony Perronti had always been, like Murphy, a backstreet guy who chased uptown girls. As it turned out, Murphy had won the grand prize and Perronti hadn't, but Murphy had thought that anything between his wife and this gangster was over and done, long ago. He'd been convinced Perronti was now either behind bars where he belonged or somewhere on the other side of the world where he didn't. But apparently not. It seemed he was not only here in Annamarie Murphy's uptown world, he was in Edwin Murphy's Cube Ergo Spa hot tub. *With* Annamarie. Good God Almighty.

"Listen to me, Maddy. This man is a career criminal, guilty of multiple felonies. He's wanted by the state police and the FBI too. They think—and I thought—he'd left the country."

"So…what are you saying?"

Murphy hesitated, thinking hard. "I'm saying I need you to go out there and hold Anthony Perronti at gunpoint until he's taken into custody. You do have a gun, right?"

"Oh yeah. Tom says always carry, just in case. But why not just call the cops?"

"I will," Murphy said. "But not the regular way. Perronti once had tight connections with the police, and maybe still does. I'll call a lawyer friend instead, somebody I trust, and he'll know which troops can safely be summoned."

"Then why don't you call the lawyer now, and I'll wait here where I am—"

"Because Perronti might leave, that's why. Is he wearing a watch?"

"Yeah. Must be waterproof."

"And he checks it every few minutes. Right?"

"Yeah, he does."

"He hasn't changed a bit. He won't be there long, I promise. And we can't risk letting him escape." In a quiet, hopefully calm voice Murphy added, "Do what I told you, and keep me on the line. After you get the drop on him, I'll make the call and send help, chop chop."

"You're the boss. But please understand, this man and your wife…well, they're—"

"Naked? Good. What better way to be sure they have no weapons?"

"Guess that makes sense," she agreed.

"There's even a reward for this bastard, and I'll make sure the reward is yours and Tom's. Understand?"

"Got it," she said. Murphy heard a moment of heavy breathing as she processed all this. Then: "What if one of them tries something?"

"They won't," he said. "Perronti's too smart to risk his life, and my wife'll be scared out of her mind. Just hold your gun on him until the cavalry arrives. You'll probably get a medal."

At that moment Murphy's office door opened and Jennifer, his assistant, stuck her head in. She saw he was occupied, pointed to his desk phone, and mouthed the words *Phones are working now*. When he nodded, she smiled and disappeared.

"You can do this, Maddy," he said, into the phone. "Do it now, and keep me connected."

"Okay."

Then Murphy heard one of the last things he expected: a soft and distant knocking sound.

"Maddy?" he said again.

"Somebody's at the front door," she hissed.

He felt his heart lurch in his chest. "Abort the plan," he said. "Go back out the window you came throu—"

"No. I'm still watching. Your wife and her friend haven't heard anything yet."

"Doesn't matter. They will soon. Get out of the house."

"Okay. You're right."

Several seconds passed. He could hear movement. "Are you clear, now?" he asked.

"No. I'm at my exit window, but two people are talking on the sidewalk in plain view."

"Dammit," he said.

Both of them fell silent. He heard more knocking. Five seconds passed. He realized he was holding the arm of his chair in a deathgrip.

"Okay, I'm at the front door now, looking through the peephole," Maddy said. "The knocker is the neighbor lady, from next door. I saw her earlier, from the car."

"Sally," he said. Busybody Sally Huxton was their only next-door neighbor. "Can you go out a different window?"

"Not without her seeing me."

Great. *What now?*

"Well, I can't let her keep knocking," Maddy said. "Maybe she can help."

"What? Wait—I don't think that's a good—"

Too late. Murphy heard the door creak open, heard her shushing the lady, inviting her in.

"What's going on?" he heard Sally Huxton ask, also in a whisper. She probably lived for stuff like this. "Is everything all right? I thought I saw someone crawl through a window—"

More hushed words. Listening hard, he realized Maddy was explaining to Sally what was happening, introducing herself, probably showing her credentials, etc. Good God. Murphy was suddenly reminded of Murphy's Law, and how true it was. He wondered if the guy who had come up with it was a distant relative.

"Maddy?" he said.

"Stay quiet," she replied. "We're doing this. I'll leave the phone on, in my shirt pocket."

Then, nothing but silence.

A very long silence.

Murphy sat there staring at the wall opposite his desk, sweat trickling down his forehead. He pictured his hired private eye and his gossippy next-door neighbor creeping through his house toward the back deck, where his wife and an old enemy were skinnydipping in a hot tub that Murphy had bought, in happier times, for one of Annamarie's birthdays. He was understandably worried, but he was also angry, and growing angrier by the minute. After all, he'd never been *certain* she was cheating. Now he knew for sure.

Then, out of nowhere, he heard a crash. Then a scream and a couple of heavy THUMPs, like a bagful of bowling balls hitting a floor. Murphy's stomach muscles clenched; he almost dropped the phone.

*"Maddy?"*

No response, and no more noise. Again, all was dead quiet.

Finally he heard a breathless voice: "Mr. Murphy? You still there?"

He knew Maddy was outside, on the deck. He'd already heard birds chirping in the background, and the rumble of faraway traffic. The interstate was only a couple hundred yards behind his house.

"What's happened, Maddy? I heard—"

"Your wife's friend wasn't happy when he saw my gun. He quick jumped up, spit out his cigarette, grabbed a flowerpot from the table beside the hot tub, and threw it at me."

"And?"

"He missed. So I whacked him with my gunbarrel, on top of his damn ugly head."

"Good God," Murphy whispered. "What'd he do then?"

"Nothing. I'm not only quiet and quick, I'm strong, too. I knocked him out."

"Did he fall back into the tub? Has he drowned?"

"No, he's lying here on the floor, wet and bleeding like a stuck hog. What a mess."

"Are you sure he's unconscious?"

"Out cold. He even banged his head again, when he hit the floor. Like the neighbor lady."

"What?"

"When he threw the flowerpot, it missed me but it hit your neighbor BOP! right on her big nose and then the pot hit the floor and broke into a hundred pieces. The neighbor lady screamed to high heaven, keeled over, and whopped her head too."

"Is she okay?"

"Well, she would be, but she landed on his lit cigarette, and her hair caught on fire."

"Oh, for God's sake—"

"She's okay now. I drug her to the side of the hot tub and dunked her head in."

Murphy tried to imagine prim and proper Sally Huxton getting her head shoved underwater—but had trouble picturing it. "What's she doing now?"

"The neighbor lady? She's sitting on the floor beside the guy, dazed and mumbling to herself. I think she's saying cuss words. Her nose is bloody and mashed flat, and some of her hair's still smoking a little."

"Okay," Murphy said. "Main thing is, watch Perronti, don't let him get up. Understand?"

"You bet." After a pause and a long breath, Maddy said, "This man, you're sure he's a criminal, right?"

"Yes, yes he's a criminal. A wanted fugitive. You did the right thing." As the thought occurred to him, Murphy said, "Where's my wife?"

Maddy swallowed loudly. "That's another story."

"What? What do you mean?"

"I mean you were right. She was scared silly. Matter of fact, she hopped right up out of the hot tub, jumped down off the deck, and took off like a scalded cat across the back yard. She keep looking back at me and ran straight into a tree trunk, but she hopped up again and kept going. She climbed over the back fence fast as a squirrel, and by the time I dunked the neighbor lady and got to the fence and through the gate your wife was running butt naked down the middle of the street. Three cars crashed into each other—*BAM!BAM!BAM!*—and lots of sidewalk people were standing there watching her with their mouths hanging open. One car turned over with its tires pointing straight up and glass everywhere and another car hit a fire plug, and now there's water gushing a million feet high and flooding the neighborhood. Last I saw of your wife, she ran right over a really old man with a walking cane and jumped on a city bus that was stopped at the corner. I bet the passengers got a big surprise out of *that*."

Murphy groaned. "Dear God, what a goat-roping." He shook his head and said, wearily, "All right, Maddy, just stay put, and watch Perronti. The cops'll be there soon, and so will I."

"Okay. While I was at the gate, two policemen ran past, chasing the bus, but they didn't stop when I tried to flag 'em down."

"Not surprising. Just remember, if Perronti moves, hit him again with your gun."

"It'd be my pleasure. What about the neighbor lady?"

"Don't worry about her," he said. "Hang on—I'll call the police on the other phone."

He picked up the landline, heard a welcome dial tone, and got lawyer Jerry Rayburn on the first ring. "Jerry? I got a situation. Remember Tony Perronti? Well, you won't believe what just—"

Murphy had a sudden thought, and stopped dead. He hung up and grabbed his cell phone.

"Maddy? A minute ago, you said my wife ran into a…tree?"

"Yeah. The big one in the middle of your yard. God that woman can run fast."

A silence passed.

"And then she ran down the street? The street bordering the interstate?"

"The street, yes. Behind your house. But I didn't see any interstate."

Murphy swallowed. Carefully he said, "This neighbor. She's tall, with black hair. Right?"

"No, she's short like me, and blond hair. Before it burned up, I mean." A pause. "What's the matter?"

Another silence, longer this time.

"Maddy?" Murphy said.

"Yessir?"

"Didn't you tell me you're at two-five-four Stanton Street?"

"Right. Two-five-four. But it's Stan*ford* Street. Two-five-four Stanford."

Silence.

"Mr. Murphy?"

Murphy disconnected, put down the cell phone, and sat for a long time staring at his new office window. When he heard his assistant's voice on his intercom, it sounded like something far away, maybe in a dream…

Dazedly, he pushed the intercom button. "What is it, Jennifer?"

"Call from your wife, sir. Line two."

Murphy punched the lit button on his desk phone, lifted the receiver, and said, in a hoarse voice, "Hello?"

"Edwin?" Annamarie said. "Well. I take it you're moved in."

He didn't reply. He couldn't seem to put his thoughts together. Beside him, his cell phone was buzzing madly; he switched it off without looking at it.

"I'm just calling to remind you we're having dinner with the Burnleys tonight," his wife said. "Edwin? Are you there?"

Murphy drew a long breath and let it out slowly. So Annamarie wasn't cheating, after all. At least not today. In a flash, his mind changed direction. A plan began to take shape.

"Remember saying we should get away for a while?" he asked her. "Far away?"

"Sure I do. How long a while?"

"I was thinking a month. No, two months."

"Really?" she said. He could picture her eyes widening. "But you've just relocated—"

"Others can cover for me. I'll call Jerry Rayburn."

"I thought Rayburn was a lawyer."

"Well, several things need covering."

"How far should we go?" she asked. "Hawaii?"

He had a sudden vision of a police station packed with angry motorists, bus passengers, an old man with a cane, two naked people, a private detective, and a woman with smoking hair. "Farther," he said. "How about Portugal?"

"Portugal?"

"An island, off the coast. Madeira. I hear it's beautiful."

"Whoa," she said, sounding pleased. "And for two months? I guess you were right, what you said about that job of yours."

"What about it?"

"It's good to be da king."

# Wanna, Wanna, Wanna
## Lesley A. Diehl

I'll admit we were kind of loud, singing at the top of our lungs as we walked arm in arm down the dark street. And we had had a lot to drink also. It was Tandy, Boogie and me, the inseparable gals trio. We were friends in high school, went to the same state college nearby and came back home to dead end jobs in the local printing plant. The pay was better than we could have earned in a larger city where our wages would have been eaten up by the cost of housing. The three of us were saving money by living at home, hoping someday to move to New York City and our dream jobs. Meantime our friendship continued, working the late shift and partying on weekends. Life was easy. We were having fun.

It was a perfect midsummer Friday night in our small upstate New York village, a place small enough that everybody knew everybody, making it difficult for the three of us to do anything too outrageous for fear someone would notify our parents. We had been drinking and dancing in our favorite local bar, The Brass Rail, where we often hung out looking for guys, not that we ever went home with one. We stayed together, on occasion giving out our phone numbers to a fella that looked promising or someone else's phone number to guys who creeped us out. I once gave the phone number of my high school nemesis to an obnoxious, drunk guy. Oddly, when the two of them hooked up they liked each other. I don't think he noticed that she wasn't the gal he met in the bar. If he did, neither of them seemed to care. They got engaged and married. He turned out to be the son of one of the wealthiest men in the county. But marriage, I told my two gal pals, wasn't always assurance of a happy life. Look at the three of us. Not as happy as we would have liked, but we were having fun.

Lights came on in the house on the corner and a man stepped out onto the front stoop and yelled at us. "I'm calling the cops."

"Run!" yelled Tandy. A high hurdler in college, she took off like an antelope closely followed by Boogie, short, pudgy, great on the dance floor, slow in a sprint. They ran back toward the center of town. Silly. The cops were sure to spot them. My choice? I grabbed the low hanging branch of a maple tree and climbed, not easy given I was wearing my red short puffy skirt with white lace around the bottom, black hose, and lace-up ankle boots, my Madonna look. I hid myself in the thick foliage. A police car pulled up in front of the house and two officers got out. The man who had summoned them came down the front steps and the three of them stood under the branch on which I was hiding.

"Mr. Hendricks," said one of the officers. "Did you recognize any of the people who made the ruckus?"

"I couldn't see them clearly, but I think they headed down that way." He pointed in the direction Tandy and Boogie had taken off.

The officers strode back to their car, and sirens wailing, took off in pursuit. Mr. Hendricks continued to stand under the tree watching them.

Oh, oh. Suddenly the booze caught up with me and I thought I might lose my balance as well as the too many beers I'd drunk. I held on and swallowed hard. Then I got the hiccups. I pressed my hand against my mouth to stifle the sound. Just when I thought nothing could get worse, I realized my bladder was full.

I looked down and could see the bald top of Mr. Hendricks' head shining in the moonlight. Oh, God. The man was in for a real surprise so much worse than being awakened by loud singing. And to add to my dismay, the police car roared up again. The officer in the passenger's seat rolled down his side window. "Couldn't find them."

"Probably a bunch of kids anyway." Hendricks stepped closer to the car. "But thanks for your help." He reached into his pocket, pulled out his wallet and extracted several bills.

"You don't have to do that. You already pay us plenty for everything else," said the officer in the passenger's seat, but he grabbed the money.

Hendricks waved the remark away and watched the cruiser drive off.

I heard a sharp crack. Mr. Hendricks heard it too and looked up. I was hidden well enough that I was certain he couldn't see me, but what I didn't count on was the branch breaking under my weight. I let go of it and fell directly on Mr. Hendricks, bouncing off his fat belly and landing next to him. He wasn't so lucky. The branch hit him on the head and knocked him unconscious.

"Mr. Hendricks?"

He didn't answer. Had I killed him? I leaned over and pressed my ear against his chest. He was still breathing. Oh, no. I saw car lights in the next block. The cops were coming by again. Time for me to scurry off before I was recognized or caught. I hobbled and hiccupped my way down the street in the direction of my friends. Home, home. I needed a bathroom.

Several streets over, Tandy and Boogie emerged from behind a house.

"Pssst," Tandy said. "Stupid move, climbing that tree."

"Maybe," I said, my thoughts torn between the signals of distress my body was sending me and what I had overheard balancing in the tree. "Maybe not."

'Let's stop at the Town Bar and have a nightcap," Tandy said. Boogie, never one to go home too early, agreed.

"Nope. That fall took it out of me." I left my two friends at the corner and ran for my parents' house and relief.

As usual, dad was in the living room watching Johnnie Carson, beer in hand and a cigarette in the full ashtray sending smoke signals onto the already yellowed wallpaper.

"Where have you been? Running around with your friends, right? Don't you want to make anything out of yourself?"

"Now what could I make of myself on a Friday night in this town?"

I tossed my purse on the table and ran for the bathroom. Ah. I flushed and met Mom on her way out of the kitchen into the living room.

"Sometimes," Mom grabbed a short puff off Dad's cigarette, "I wish she'd stay out with other than those girlfriends. Don't you like boys?"

"Not the boys I meet."

"Try meeting fellas somewhere else other than at a bar," Mom suggested.

"Where?"

"At church, maybe?" she replied.

"The guys at church are the same one at the bars, Mom. G'night." I gave her a peck on the cheek and closed the door to my room.

Sleep was slow to come. I had heard and seen something that night that I knew wasn't right, something that involved the police and Mr. Hendricks. I had to find out what it meant—a change in my routine that sounded like…well, fun.

* * *

"Do we know the Hendricks' family?" The next morning, Sunday, I sat with my parents at the kitchen table drinking coffee and picking at an English muffin.

"No family that I know of, only Mr. Hendricks. He moved here last year and took the position of controller for the town government. Why so curious?" My mother refilled my cup and dumped my muffin crumbs in the garbage.

"I hear he's looking for a part-time assistant in his office, but I don't suppose you'd be interested in that, would you? Just willing to work the line in the bindery and run around with those friends of yours. Why did I pay for four years of college?" Dad lit up the first of his cigarettes for the day. "Never thought women should go to college anyway."

"Tell you what, Dad. I think I'll mosey down to the town office building on Monday and see about that job."

Dad almost choked on his coffee and looked shocked.

* * *

Before my plant shift, which began at three in the afternoon, I walked into Mr. Hendricks's office and told his secretary I wanted to apply for the job opening. I wore my best teal and dark green dress, mid length, shoulder pads almost to my ear lobes and a pair of platform espadrilles. My grown-up, business look.

"No appointment?" Mrs. Fleming patted her heavily sprayed and teased coiffure and peered over the rims of her glasses at me.

I looked around the room. It was empty. "I didn't know there would be a waiting line for an interview."

"Watch your tone, young lady." But her mouth curved upward in a smile. "You're kind of sassy, just what this office needs. Got a resume?"

I handed her the single sheet of paper I'd typed up earlier this morning.

"So I see you've had some job experience." She glanced over the paper.

"How many other applicants have there been?" I asked.

"You're the first."

"Not much competition then,"

"Not much of a job either. Pay's lousy, but it will be a step up from the printing plant." She gestured to a chair. "Sit. I'll let him know you're here." She knocked on the inner office door and stuck her head in. "A Miss Dawson to see you about the job opening."

She handed my resume back to me and gestured for me to enter.

Hendricks stood up. Yup, same man from Saturday night. Belly bulging over his belt, bald head with a large bandage just above his right ear and one eye swollen and turning black.

"Mr. Hendricks, are you okay? I can come back."

"No, no. Just a little accident. I was trimming some trees and a branch fell on me."

So I knew the man could tell half the truth, but not all of it.

I handed him my resume. He stumbled backward, grabbed his desk chair to steady himself, sank into the seat and began to peruse the page.

"A degree in English literature, huh? Not much of a call for that in today's job market, is there?"

"No, but I have numerous job experiences as you can see. Plus I'm a fast learner." Now I was lying. When I first began working at the printing plant, I was assigned the mailing room, where I was supposed to read mailing labels on magazines moving down a conveyer belt, grab all the magazines with the same zip code off the belt, feed them to a binder and stack them on a wooden skid. I found it impossible to read the moving labels.

"Are you illiterate?" the foreman yelled. "A college graduate and you can't read a simple five number zip code?"

"Usually my textbooks remained still on my desk. Things are easier to read that way." I knew I shouldn't have mouthed off and would pay for it somehow. The next night I was moved to the bindery where all I had to do was fill hoppers with catalogue parts, no reading required, and of course, lower pay.

Mr. Hendricks pulled off his glasses and propped them on his head. "Your work experience is a bit odd. It says here you worked in college in the psychology department's animal lab. What did you do there?"

"Scraped rat shit."

Hendricks raised his swollen eyebrow and peered at me through bloodshot eyes.

"My work experience is diverse, so I adjust well to any job. As you can see, I worked for one summer in the local publishing house."

"That's good, but I don't see a job title here."

"That would be 'stripper.'"

He cleared his throat and appeared about to get out of his chair and dismiss me.

"Really, it's an official job title. I stripped the covers off unsold paperbacks that drug stores and supermarkets had purchased from publishers. Our local publishing company served as an intermediary for those publishers. The stripped covers were sent back to the publishers for money. We took a percentage of the money while another percentage went back to the stores that returned the books."

"What happened to the books?"

"Landfill. They couldn't be sold without the covers, but…"

"But?" For the first time since I stepped into his office, he sat forward in his chair and looked interested.

"But I believe the boss of the stripping division sold some of them to secondhand bookstores."

"That didn't bother you, that he broke the law?"

I shrugged my shoulders. "I had no proof he did. What could I do?"

Hendricks looked pleased with my answer. He settled back in his chair, folded his arms across his stomach and interlocked his fingers. "Our office deals with sensitive matters, government information, you know, important papers that shouldn't be shared outside this building. Do you think you could handle that?"

"Oh sure. I know lots of things about people around here and I don't blab it all over town."

"What people?" His jaw dropped and he seemed worried about what I might say.

"I can't tell you, can I, or you'd think I was lying about not gossiping about what I knew?" I gave him a snarky little smile.

He hesitated a minute and appeared to roll around in his head what I had told him. This time he got out of his chair, smiled and said, "The job's yours. When can you start?"

* * *

I resigned from my position at the printing plant that afternoon. The pay in Mr. Hendrick's office wasn't any higher than at the plant, but the work conditions were better, no paper dust in the air or ear shattering noises from the bindery machines, and my curiosity had been piqued by overhearing Mr. Hendricks' and the police officers' conversation the other night. When I told my parents about my new job, they approved. To them it appeared I wanted to move into a better position. When I told Tandy and Boogie, they were less than thrilled.

"You've sold us out," said Tandy. "I thought the three of us would work at the plant until we could get enough money together to all move to the city, get an apartment and work our way into jobs that held the promise of promotion."

So I told them about what I had overheard between Hendricks and the officers.

"So what? You're going to get yourself into a lot of trouble, if you nose around, you know," said Boogie.

"Not if you two help me if I get in a tight spot. Have I ever cut the two of you out of anything I was involved in?"

"So we're all going to be spies then," said Boogie.

"Not spies. More like undercover operatives."

Tandy giggled. "We'll be like a special police unit taskforce."

"Except we're not police. The police may be the ones we need to investigate. You two keep your ears and eyes open at the printing plant. The employees there may have heard rumors."

"What will you be doing?' asked Tandy.

"I'll try to go through Mr. Hendricks office and…"

"And you'll also be in a position to chat with the police Chief, Lanny Montrose." Boogie grinned. "Wasn't he sweet on you in high school?" She paused and her giggle turned to a frown. "Is that why you wanted to take this job? So you could flirt with Chief Montrose?"

"No, absolutely not," But I did like that idea. On the other hand, what if Lanny was in on whatever was going on between the cops and Hendricks? I'd have to be sly and clever. What fun.

* * *

On my first day working with Mr. Hendricks I learned he spent most of his time drinking coffee in the town office's break room with the other employees. Because the police department was housed on the ground floor, one flight down from Hendrick's office, and the jail in the basement of the building, I saw everyone come and go and, after several weeks at my job, I learned the routine of all the town officials and the police officers and knew when Lanny liked to take a midmorning break for coffee. I watched him pull out of the lot early each morning, a smile on his face, and pull back into the lot at ten, the smile still there. Lanny loved to be in his cruiser. If there was anything illegal going on, it was unlikely Lanny knew about it because he was always out in the patrol car.

Let me tell you about Lanny. Sure, he was handsome. Sure, he was the high scorer for the basketball team in high school. And sure, he had been elected home coming king our junior and senior years of high school. But according to the school yearbook editors, they puzzled over what label they could use under his picture. I understood there were some unkind titles contemplated such as "least likely to graduate until the millennium" and "only guy to fail women's volleyball." Instead, the caption under his picture read, "Knows the rules of the road by heart." And he did. Ask him about caution signs, warning signs and regulatory signs, speed limits on county versus state roads, DUIs, speeding tickets, anything to do with tires on pavement and Lanny could quote the appropriate regulation word for word. Lanny liked rules, which he once told me, made living clear and straightforward. Lanny did not like gray areas, not in areas of work and, as I soon found out, not in social settings.

My working for the village government gave Lanny and me the opportunity to renew our acquaintance begun years ago in high school. On our third date, following an expensive steak dinner and a movie and parked in my parents' drive, Lanny leaned in close. "I know why you're spending so much time with me."

"You do?"

"Oh, yes. You want something from me. And I'm willing to give it to you."

My heart went thump, thump, thump as I looked into the soft brown eyes of this 6-foot, 2-inch hunk of man.

He leaned closer to me and whispered in my ear. "You're a gal after my own heart. We could be good together."

"Yes?"

I turned toward him and closed my eyes for the kiss I expected to come.

"So, I'm willing to put a good word in for you after you take the exam. You could move up in the ranks in the police department and be a lieutenant in a few months."

Nope. This fellow was not a bent cop. He was still Lanny, the rules and regulations guy.

My eyes popped open, and I searched for a reply. "Actually, Lanny. I'm not a woman who likes to work under anybody. I was thinking more in the line of private investigator." Was I? Was that a career path for me, from working the bindery to detective? Hmmmm.

"Yeah, I can see that. The cops' uniforms don't fit women well."

No, they don't, in so many ways.

"So here's the thing, Lanny. I think some of your cops and Mr. Hendricks may not be following the rules."

Now that got his attention.

"Who? I'll arrest them first thing tomorrow morning," said my by-the-book police chief.

"I appreciate your confidence in me, but I don't even know what crime is being committed. I suspect the police and Mr. Hendricks are up to something, but I'll have to look around Mr. Hendricks' office. We need evidence, you know."

"Right!" Lanny's face lit up. "Evidence. You get some for me and then I'll make the arrests."

The knowledge that Lanny might soon be arresting some criminals made his night as neither a kiss nor a steak dinner could.

The other two members of my spy organization heard rumors at the plant that two officers had been in the local pool hall bragging about a "sweet deal" they had going on with Hendricks. Of course the willingness of the two cops to spread around a lot of money among the guys at the bar meant no one there was willing to say much else about their pals' newfound windfall. But Tandy and Boogie learned the names of two cops in on whatever criminal enterprise Hendricks had created.

* * *

The morning after I had talked with Lanny about Hendricks and the cops, when Hendricks left for his coffee break, I went into his office and began to go through his desk drawers and the filing cabinets there. When I pulled out the bottom drawer of one of the cabinets, I discovered the drawer full of packages of what looked like powder wrapped in cellophane bags. Drugs of some sort, probably heroin. I was about to nab one of the packets to bring to Lanny when I heard the outer office door open and Mr. Hendricks speaking to someone. I quietly closed the cabinet and stood there hoping my face gave away nothing of my snooping.

"What are you doing here, in my private office?" Mr. Hendricks face was dark with suspicion.

"Uh, I thought you'd carried the monthly report in here and left it on your desk, but I couldn't find it."

"It's in my desk." Hendricks walked over to his desk and pulled the report from the top drawer. "Here you go."

I smiled. "Thanks."

I started toward the door, but Hendricks grabbed my arm. "And don't ever come in here again without my permission." He continued to grip my arm tightly. "Understand?"

"Yes." I fled out the door and told Mrs. Fleming I would be in the break room getting coffee.

The only way I could accuse Hendricks was to grab the packets and turn them over to Lanny. And I had to be quick about it. How could I get him out of the office, go back in and grab the evidence? My gaze traveled the hallway walls, desperate for anything that would suggest a plan. And then I saw it. The fire alarm. So, of course, I pulled it.

The loud distress signal had everyone in the hall running for the exits. Instead I dashed up the back stairs, meeting only Mrs. Fleming on her way down.

"I left my purse in the office. It had money and my driver's license in it. I've got to get it."

I continued up the stairs. She hesitated for a minute then continued down the stairs. "Silly girl."

I rushed into the office where I ran into Mr. Hendricks standing in front of his office door.

"You need to get out of here," I urged. "There's a fire."

"I don't think so." He gave me a devil's grin. "I finally got around to removing that tree limb that fell in my front yard several weeks ago and found this." He held out a scrap of white cotton lace material. "I believe it matches the tear in that skirt you sometimes wear, the one you've got on today."

I didn't bother looking down at the hem of my skirt, knowing that he was right. I tried to slip past him out the door into the hallway, but the two officers whom I had seen the night I hid in the tree stood there.

"Grab the goods," said Hendricks. "I'll take care of missy here." He rushed me down the back stairs and the officers followed. Outside in the parking lot, Henricks shoved me into the back of his car and the officers got into one of the patrol cars and left.

Hendricks followed.

"You'll never get away with this, you know." I tried the door, but he had set the child safety locks on the back doors.

"Shut up."

As we sped out the gravel drive, we narrowly missed Lanny's car entering. I couldn't tell if he saw me in Hendricks' car or not, but it was my only hope to be saved.

"Don't think he'll follow us. He has responsibilities at the station. You know how seriously he takes his position. Guy never suspected anything because he spent all his time in the field." Henricks sneered and added, "Idiot."

Hendricks pulled up in front of his house, disengaged the door locks and reached into the back seat to pull me out. I slid across the seat and exited the other side of the car. I yelled as I fled down the sidewalk but realized no one was at home during the day to hear me. I ran around the back of his house, but Hendricks was hot on my heels, so close I could smell the coffee on his breath. Wow. This fat little guy was fast. A few more steps and he would catch me.

I quickly looked around for an escape route. Ah, well. I did it once.

Why not again? I began scrambling up the tree. Hendricks looked up and shook his fist at me. "Come down here, you little shit."

I climbed higher.

Hendricks grabbed one of the lower branches and started after me. I looked down, not wanting to climb higher because I intended to jump to the ground and continue running. I felt a hand close around my foot. I kicked at his face, a move that catapulted him out of the tree and sent me plummeting after him. And again, I bounced off that fat belly and onto the ground. This time Hendricks was not so lucky. The tree limb, weakened by both our weights came down next, landing next to me but hitting Hendricks and knocking him out…again. Trees and Hendricks did not get along.

I heard a car pull to the curb. I looked up and saw the police department logo on the door. Oh, no. Hendricks' two cop buddies.

"Okay, hands up. You're under arrest for attempted murder."

I pushed my way through the foliage with my hands in the air.

"Not, you. Him." Lanny had his gun out and aimed at Hendricks.

Hendricks came to and let out a squeal of pain.

"Why are you here?" I asked Lanny.

"I saw Briggs and Bolles racing down the road out of town and wondered what they were up to. All police personnel should have been at the station because of the fire. I stopped them and they told me everything. I arrested them, found Hendricks' briefcase in the car with the drugs and decided to see if I could apprehend him at his house. I see you did it for me. Very brave of you."

"It's what I do."

Lanny looked puzzled.

"I'm good at tree climbing. He's not."

Hendricks let out a groan. "Hey, you two. I need medical help here. Could you call an ambulance? I'm in a lot of pain. And I want to press charges. She tried to kill me."

"Did she?" Lanny said.

Hendricks tried to crawl away, but Lanny put his foot on Hendricks' leg to prevent him from moving.

"I'd better call the station and get help."

"I'm fine." I said.

"He doesn't mean you. He means help for me." Hendricks continued to squirm and writhe.

"What did he do to you?" asked Lanny, placing his hand on my shoulder.

"Chased me up a tree."

"And that's not even close to attempted murder!" yelled Hendricks.

"Here's the story. I overheard him talking several weeks ago to those two officers. I knew he was up to something. Then I searched his office and found those drugs in his file cabinet, but he caught me. He sent the officers off with the drugs and he threw me in his car. I think he meant to get rid of me."

Lanny took my hand and led me to his car, opened the door and I slid in. Lanny got in and started the engine.

"Hey, what about me?" Hendricks yelled.

"Help should be here soon. Don't move." Lanny put the car in gear, and we drove off.

* * *

Lanny wanted me to stay in town, again telling me what a good officer I would make. It was tempting, but I knew my future wasn't here. Tandy, Boogie and I had gotten as much out of this town as we could, so we decided it was time we made our move. We pooled our savings to head for the Big Apple where we intended to rent a cheap apartment together and find jobs. You know, a bigger city where we could have fun in so many more ways, ways we had yet to imagine. Cuz, you know, girls just wanna have fun.

# Marge and Dot Go Rogue
## Sandra Murphy

I'd barely turned the corner at Maple and Second when I saw Dot halfway down her sidewalk, headed for the curb. Most times, I have to wait while she made sure she'd unplugged the toaster, didn't leave the stove on although she's a total microwaver, and the kitchen sink wasn't overflowing. She always does a quick check at the door—keys, backup keys, phone, glasses, purse, and bra. Then, she felt ready. You'd think we were on the way to meet royalty instead of headed to the library. Given the romance novels she read, she met her fair share of Prince Charmings on the page, but there she was, yanking on the door before I got the car in Park.

"What's the hurry? Isn't today oatmeal raisin cookies and Earl Grey tea? Not something I'd rush for."

"It was supposed to be, but Alma called, all upset the cookies burned themselves into hockey pucks. What really happened is that cute neighbor of hers cut the grass with his shirt off and she lost track of time. She wasn't so much in an uproar over the cookies but that someone would find out she ogled the guy." Dot slammed the car door with a bit more force than necessary and glared at me. "Sue Ann stepped up and made lemon drizzle cupcakes, the little bitty ones. You can have a lot of them before they mount up to the same calories as a big cupcake. Scientific fact. Are we going or just going to sit here?"

Ours is not a large library but it's filled with avid readers. The kid section is alive with volunteers dressed as characters from the books they read aloud to the age impaired, also known as five-year-olds. Now and again, the activities director brings in a cooking demonstration for the adults who share the resulting food. If a dish can't be completed in the scheduled amount of time, like when the BBQ King made us drool over his description of sliders with a side of charred peaches or the day we learned how to make a Baked Alaska, the guest would bring generous samples to pass around. Except one time. Chef Andre gave a long lecture about how wonderful a chef he was, how wonderful his food was, and how wonderful it was he came to mingle with the little people, which meant us, the not famous. Meanwhile, our heads swiveled, in search of helpers and a table of samples. There were none. When the talk ended at last, Chef Andre invited us to buy a copy of his cookbook/autobiography, autographed for free, usually a $50 surcharge. He happened to have fifty copies with him. Incensed at the insult of no food, we all declined. Chef Andre went home with fifty autographed copies and a bad attitude. As Dot said, he would have been better off to have brought amuse bouche and lots of them.

Today's topic was 'Write what you know vs what you can research'. I wondered if there would be snacks. I both know, and can research, snacks.

Dot and I first met when we both worked at the library. I was in charge of the mystery/thriller section; she took care of romance books. Through crossover titles, mysteries with romance storylines, we became best friends. Now retired, we still attended library programs to show support and help out where we could.

The library is only two miles from Dot's house so we arrived in no time and found prime parking two over from the reserved handicap spot. "I want to see if they have the newest romance." Dot grinned. "I don't remember the name, but the cover is blue." It cracked us up after so many years of similar requests from patrons.

"I want a CD, I don't remember the song or singer, but it goes like this." I hummed a few bars of out of tune, non-rhythmic notes and laughed some more. We'd heard that one lots of times too. Librarian humor, gotta love it.

We were mid-snicker when we walked into the main room. Dot gasped and grabbed my arm for support. My mouth hung open in shock. Two patrons ran into us from behind and we didn't even notice.

Half the shelves were empty and sobbing employees continued to pull out more books and stack them on carts.

"What's going on? Where are the books?" I could barely get the questions out.

Sally, she's in charge of mysteries now, answered. "With the new laws the state passed, people can object to books they think are inappropriate and we have to take them off the shelf rather than corrupt a child or teenager's mind. Or an adult too, I guess." Tears ran down her cheeks. "Worse yet, the city council skimmed the titles, didn't even look at the books or back cover blurbs to find out what they're about. We have been ordered to destroy books. All the 'objectionable' ones. No recourse." She pulled a tissue from her sleeve, wiped her face, and blew her nose with the sound of a honking goose flying overhead. "Romances because of love scenes and mysteries because of murders or other crimes. Sci fi because it's fantasy. Poetry is frivolous. Destroy them? We'll be reduced to a John Deere tractor repair manual from 1956 on the shelf. Solo." Sally began to hiccup. She pointed to the manual, the cover a close up of a faded green tractor.

"Um, Sally, hate to tell you but if they're that picky, the manual will have to go too." Dot shook her head. "I spent summers at my aunt and uncle's farm. The little thingys on the side there, those are called nipples."

"Surely the children's book are safe, right?" One of the women who came in behind us asked. Molly, I think her name is. "I mean what can be wrong with Humpty Dumpty, Cinderella, Sleeping Beauty, The Three Bears?"

"Humpty disobeyed safety protocols and fell, Cinderella's prince was basically a stalker, Sleeping Beauty shows stepmothers in a bad light, and the Three Bears show Goldielock's sense of privilege the way she let herself into their home, ate and criticized their food and furniture. Nothing is safe."

"What's the deadline? Is there time to fight this asinine decision?" I was furious. The library is the heartbeat of the town. What is life without imagination?

"Monday morning, there's a truck coming to take them to the incinerator."

We'd gathered a small group by then and tongues wagged at warp speed. "No one can tell me what I can and cannot read." "I can't afford to buy new books. What will I do?" "Where will my kid study after school? There won't be anything left for him to read." "I heard a town even banned cookbooks." At our inquiring looks, the woman explained, "They objected to the word 'breast' so, you know, chicken breasts got swept up in the ban, no matter it makes no sense. There's always somebody who is offended by everything." Overall, there were a lot of banned curse words used to describe the city council and state legislature.

The day's guest speaker said, "No point in talking about what you can research. One town banned dictionaries and restricted access to search engines! Let's talk about how to fix this."

At the end of the hour, we were no farther along with ideas but planned to meet again. We'd also enlisted the high school kids to picket after school. Loudly. In front of television cameras, and cell phones to post on Instagram, and Tik Tok.

At five, I drove Dot home. We didn't talk much on the way, all talked out after the meeting, I guess.

"I'll call you tomorrow. We'll think of something. We have to." Dot got out of the car and walked to her house a lot slower than she'd come to the curb earlier.

My cell phone rang before I could pull away. "Marge? It's Mal, can you come by? Have I got a deal for you!"

I was only blocks away from Mal's so I said yes. In a small town, most anything is only blocks away from where you are and where you want to be. Less than five minutes later, I pulled into Mal's parking lot. The car stuttered and farted black smoke from the tailpipe.

"What took you so long? You coulda walked faster than that thing went." Mal waved the smoke away.

"There was a traffic jam. Brownie Troop 463 were told to use the crosswalk and go single file. They dawdle. Who knew we had so many Brownies in town? When those kids get older, there will be a cookie sales war." I patted my car on its fanny, also known as the rear fender. "We did the best we could."

"That's what I wanted to talk to you about. I'm teaching an after-school class to kids who want to learn how to take care of their own cars, before everything goes electric. Somebody's going to have to drive the older models or the country will sink under the weight of rusted gas powered rejects." Mal walked as fast as she talked and was almost at the corner of the building before I passed the restroom, the halfway point. "I thought it would be good for the kids, and for you, if we used your car for our lessons. You'll get a repaired car, no charge, and the kids get experience."

"What am I supposed to drive in the meantime? Walking is good for my health but I'm not apt to walk everywhere, especially with bags of groceries." I was a little out of breath already. Maybe I did need to walk more often.

She veered left around the back. "I've got something you won't be able to resist."

I almost bumped into her when she made an abrupt stop. Her big grin said I'd either love it or hate it, always a toss up with Mal.

With a flourish and a ta-da, she moved out of the way and I turned the corner to see…an ice cream truck. An ice cream truck with an especially bright pink scoop of ice cream on a waffle cone mounted on the roof. "It still plays music. What do you think?"

"I think I'd have herds of kids chasing me down the street when all I was doing was going to buy bananas. Where in the world did this come from?"

"You remember Freddy, right? He retired to Florida, is thinking of coming back, too hot and too many old people down there he says. Like he's a spring chicken. Even if he comes back, he won't want to jump behind the wheel right away. It's the perfect solution."

Her grin spread ear to ear. I needed a tactful way to say oh hell no without hurting her feelings. Nothing came to mind.

"Come on, I'll show you the inside. There are shelves, storage, and the freezers of course. I remember you told me once, you always wanted to be the bookmobile lady. Here's your chance."

I did my best to smile but it must have wobbled and she saw it. "I'm sorry Marge, I just dumped this on you without thinking ahead. The problem is, the scrap yard cars are all pretty much skeletons, the parts being sold off piece by piece. I let it slip to the students we'd have a car in need of a fix up but still drivable and they're so excited. It gets them out of study hall for one thing. Never you mind, I'll think of something else to do. Maybe a computer simulation."

"No, no, don't say anything yet. It just took me by surprise, that's all. The car does need multiple repairs and retirement budgets don't go as far as they should." I straightened my shoulders and swallowed the sigh that threatened to come out. "Give me a day or so to think about it. I could maybe lay in a lot of frozen dinners, non-perishables, like that, keep my trips to a minimum. How long would you have the car?"

"Um, well, maybe all summer? I know it's a lot to ask but each class is for three weeks and there are four classes, all full."

Mal looked so down, just thinking about it, I said, "Let me take a look. We'll go for a test drive. You can chase off the herds of kids if they stampede after us. I haven't driven anything this big in a long while."

After our truck tour and three laps around town, without kid's screams for us to stop, I went home for dinner. My stomach made sounds of protest as the library's mini lemon cupcakes had disappeared from its memory. A tuna salad on wheat bread, green grapes, and salt and vinegar chips meal later, my stomach was full of food and my mind full of questions about the book ban.

Dot must have been on the same wavelength because she called as I rinsed my plate and glass. "The Friends of the Library are meeting tomorrow at one o'clock. At the library, of course. Can you pick me up?"

"I'll be there at 12:30. I expect there'll be a crowd."

* * *

I was right on that count. The Friends brought friends, kids cut class, and three retirement homes delivered vans full of oldsters who relied on the library and its computers to keep up to date on current events, national news, and photo updates from their families. The local television station had a camera person and reporter on hand. I felt bad for the reporter, Sherri Lynn, as she interviewed a crying four-year-old

90

girl. "They gonna burn *Bun, Bun, Bernie and His Two Mommies*," she sobbed. "My favorite book. It has bunnies on the front. Now Robbie at preschool sez two mommies is bad!"

Sherri Lynn survived the kid but went three shades pale when the cane and walker crowd stalked after her. They gave her an earful that would take up the whole six o'clock news. It's a small town. If it was a slow news day, the kind we most often have, she might get away with it. Dot and I laid odds the affiliates would pick up the Bun Bun clip. It would go viral on YouTube in fifteen minutes, tops.

After an hour and a half of talk, most of the little kids and some of the pensioners had dozed off. The teens were restless until colored markers and posterboard was distributed for protest signs. They showed great imagination and creativity.

I asked a question toward the end of the meeting. "Why can't you just give the books to us? We'll keep them safe, swap them around to read, until this craziness is over with. There's no need to ever burn books."

Sally answered. "Remember, our books are stamped with the library's name, in several places. If you were caught with one, you could be arrested. What's left of the library would be shut down. They have to be destroyed according to the council's ruling. The next council meeting is a month away. It's too late. They refused our request for an emergency meeting."

It was a sad but cursing crowd that left the library.

"Mal called after I dropped you off yesterday," I said. "Let's run by there so you can see the surprise she sprung on me. If that doesn't cheer you up, at least for a few minutes, nothing will." Despite Dot's pleas, I didn't give her any clues except to say we'd ride in style for once.

At Mal's Garage and Snacks, I told Dot to tie a scarf over her eyes so she couldn't peek. She grumbled a lot but did it. I led her to the back of the building and said, "You can look now."

Seeing Dot with her mouth wide open but unable to say anything was the highpoint of my day so far. Mal had to lean against the building, she laughed so hard.

"Uh…I…what the hell?"

"This is my new ride. Mal's got four classes of wannabe mechanics signed up and you know my car is in need of more repairs than my budget will cover. This is the 'loaner car' she's letting me drive in the meantime." I grabbed Dot's hand and pulled her to the truck. "Look inside. We'll be able to go to those thrift stores you like and buy more than knickknacks. We could get small tables and spruce them up to sell at the flea market. What do you think?"

Dot stared, stunned but seemed to recover after a few minutes. She ran her hand over the shelving, sized up the cabinets and open area, and then walked around the outside four times before she spoke. "Mal, any of them kids you got artistic?"

"I'm sure there's several. Do you want a new paint job, something not ice creamy? I hope you don't want flames and dragons!"

"No, I want a giant pair of sunglasses for the cone to wear. Can you do that?"

"Damn, Dot, you always manage to surprise me. I imagine I can. Dark frames and lenses? Something fancy with rhinestones?"

"Like the Blues Brothers wore. That's what it needs. As soon as you can, please." With that, Dot grabbed my shoulder and shoved me all the way back to the car. "Drive! To the library!"

"We just came from there. This was fun, now you want to go back to that dreary place and get sad all over again?"

"I got an idea. Now, be quiet and drive as fast as this old bucket will go. I've got some thinking to do." She refused to say another word and when asked, just shook her head.

We had to stop at the red light, the only stoplight in town. Dot spoke then. "Pull in to the Dairy Queen. I'm in need of a blizzard." Fortified by sugar, chocolate syrup, and cold creaminess, we were back at the library ten minutes later. "Go get Sally and bring her out here, please. This can't go any farther yet."

Mysterious doesn't begin to describe Dot when she's in one of her moods. Given her background in romance novels, it always caught me off guard. I obeyed.

"Hey, Dot. If you're here to check out a book before Monday's deadline,

I'm not allowed to help you. They have to be boxed and ready to go on time." Sally leaned against the fender and lifted her face to the sun, eyes closed.

"Tell us again about the library marking the books."

Sally looked puzzled but said, "We have a rubber stamp with the library's name on it, almost an inch tall. Stamp it on the inkpad, then on the edge of the pages when the book is closed, on the top edge, on the block, you know. There are also smaller ones inside the front or back covers. And an anti-theft strip hidden inside the book so it won't leave without being checked out. Of course, we're removing those as we pack, not sure if they'd burn." Her voice broke on that last word. "Why are you asking? You know all of this from when you worked here."

"Just checking to see if there's been any updates to the system. So…if I'm seen around town reading a book with the Bunker Bay Library stamp on it, we'd all be in trouble, is that it? But if I had that same title, without the library's name on it, no one could do anything about it, right?"

"Well, yeah, but you can't remove the stamp from the book, that's the whole point."

Dot revealed her plan. We thought it just might work.

* * *

Sally took her lunch hour, not that there were many people in the library. After all, there were no longer many books in the library either. We made the trek back to Mal's and showed Sally the ice cream truck. She took it better than Dot had.

After we measured the cabinets, storage areas, and freezers, Sally stated it was a wild, unrealistic, and off the wall idea. She stared at the truck for long seconds and then said, "Sunglasses?"

"To let people know we're on a mission, like the Blues Brothers. Also, we're not selling ice cream. Otherwise, we'd attract the wrong crowd and too much attention. This way we might get hungry kids but hungry for books, not cones. A casual observer would never suspect. Marge picked out a song for the thing to play, not a kid's song. Something appropriate." Dot grinned. "Are you in? It could get you in a lot of trouble."

"Plausible deniability, Dot, plausible deniability. I'm all in. I'll call ahead for you and make sure each stop does the same. Sunday night, after dark. Be there."

* * *

As a student of mystery and crime books, I knew to dress all in black. Sally had disabled the light over the loading dock where the books were boxed and stacked, ready to transport to the incinerator. Players from the high school sports teams agreed to load the boxes and never speak of it. We didn't even have to threaten them, just mentioned it was a covert mission to benefit the library.

Boxes were hidden in freezer compartments, storage, and the smaller ones were strapped onto shelves. Dot and I had mentioned to one or two of the town's biggest gossips we were on vacation for a few weeks and hinted at a destination in the opposite direction of what we had in mind.

"Now when you get to Otter Hill, go to the motel, room seven. The key will be under the mat. Tomorrow, cruise through town with music playing and stop for breakfast at DeLore's Diner. When you leave, park behind the diner and open for business. For night instructions, ask for Bernice."

"Got it. If each library follows instructions, we should be good to keep going." I leaned forward and gave Sally a hug. "Use your best sad but sincere face when you are shocked, shocked I say, the books have disappeared, must have been thieves who thought they were getting something of value."

"You are getting true valuables. I won't have to act sad. I'll miss you two but I'm so grateful you're saving the books. See you in a couple of weeks."

With tearful waves and see-you-soons, we drove into the night.

* * *

Room seven was roomy and clean with beds that vibrated if you put a quarter in the slot. Dot had to try hers out several times, laughing as it shook, as much from relief we'd made it out of town as at the silliness of the bed. "Do you think they'll be ready for us in the morning?"

"I do. Sally called Bernice and she's all set. Let's get some rest so we can take care of this and get out of town before anybody catches on."

The plan was simple enough. If citizens of Bunker Bay couldn't have books with Bunker Bay Library stamped on them, we'd give the books to residents of Otter Hill. In turn, Otter Hill Library would give us their banned books and we'd head to Wolves Way to swap again. No one would have books that had been banned from their own libraries. Librarians knew to look for us at a diner for breakfast and the ice cream truck was easy to spot. City councils were enraged books had been stolen but given 'these economic times' who could be shocked? That was the story and we all stuck to it.

We rode high on success until after the sixth swap. A sheriff had spoken to the sheriff a town over and mentioned missing books. What a coincidence, that sheriff had the same problem. Soon, they began to unravel the plan. At the diner of town seven, a waitress passed us a note to let us know.

"What do you think we ought to do?" I was worried but also furious we'd had to resort to such dealings to save beloved books.

"We've about covered this county, just three more to go. The librarians here phoned ahead, so it's set up. The plan spread to other counties, we're not working alone anymore. Let's do it and then go home for a while. Maybe those imbecile city council members have grown a brain. Doubtful, but one can hope."

"Agreed. After all, who would arrest a couple of little old ladies in an ice cream truck?" I gave Dot my best befuddled little old lady look and cracked her up.

* * *

I spoke too soon. The next day, before we even got to Arrowhead Township, I heard the *whoop whoop* of a siren behind us. I pulled over and tried to think what to say. I knew we hadn't been speeding. The problem was, we were conspicuous. "Be chill, Dot. We got this." My voice only wobbled a bit.

"License and registration, please." The officer wore a wide-brimmed hat, mirrored sunglasses, and had a small moustache. I handed over the items without a remark or a glance his way. He walked back to his patrol car to check us out.

Ten minutes later, he came back, laughing all the way. "Well, gag me with a spoon, Miz Marge, what have you got yourself into now?"

This time I looked at his name tag, did a double take on his face, and laughed too. "Robbie Mackintire, you're a cop? After all the times you were in detention at school, I'd never have believed it."

"Is that Miz Dot with you? I should have known. What's this about the two of you bootlegging?"

"Come around back."

We gave him the tour and the backstory to go with it. "Damn, people in office don't seem to have a lick of common sense once they're elected. I tell you what, I'll give you an escort into town, eat breakfast with you if that's okay. It'll let the townies know we know and we're cool with it. When you leave, I'll escort you to the city limits and hand you off to another department."

"You'd do that? They'd do that? Why? We won't be arrested for stealing?"

"You bailed me out on term papers. Cops in small towns have more downtime than city cops so a good book is good company. Who doesn't like a McBain or Parker to fill the time on a long shift?" He patted the truck's door. "The librarians gave you those books, no stealing involved. No money's changing hands. Nothing to see here. I don't know how fast this buggy can go but I'll keep you in the rearview, okay?"

"Robbie, Mal souped this buggy up, fast enough moonshiners could outrun revenuers. Open wide up, lights and sirens, we'll try not to pass you."

"Yes, ma'am!"

"We need some runnin' with the law music, don't you think?" Dot reached for the radio dial.

"I cued it up on the CD player, ready for times just like this."

Robbie pulled alongside, red, white, and blue flashers blazing, siren warming up.

"Hit it, Dot!"

We peeled out to Glen Frey's *The Heat Is On* at full volume and didn't look back.

Never underestimate a librarian.

# That Damn Car!
## Shari Held

"Kip, that's car theft. The cops could arrest us for that."

Kip kicked the threadbare tire on the station wagon he'd inherited from his mom and stared at the candy apple red Claymore Cougar kissing the curb across the street. "Chill out, Ron. It's not theft if it's my brother's car. Mom won't let Berger turn us in. Besides, when will we ever get a chance to drive such an awesome automobile?"

He had a point. The car in front of Charla Sue's duplex was rad to the max. The sleek performance model sported pop-up headlights, tailfins, and a snarling cougar hood ornament. It was keyless, and Kip dangled the key fob in front of me like the Pied Piper luring me into following him as he crossed the street and stood in front of his temptation.

I cracked my knuckles to help me think. I'm no legal whiz, just your average high school graduate, but I wasn't as confident as Kip that we wouldn't be charged with theft. Mrs. Berrettini doted on Berger, who was seven years older than us and an engineer for Claymore, a fancy-schmancy boutique car manufacturer fifty miles north of Indianapolis. The smug yuppie in his power suits rarely acknowledged the two of us in our usual uniform of logo sweatshirts (Coca-Cola for me and Nike for Kip), Jordache jeans, and Reeboks.

"Don't take this the wrong way, but Berger still hasn't forgiven you for dyeing his new Calvin Klein college underwear pink. You really want to risk it?"

"It's no big deal. I only need it long enough for Paula to see me and say 'yes' when I ask her out for tomorrow night." He nodded at the sad-sack station wagon. "Cruisin' around in that old thing isn't gonna hack it. I'll schmooze her in Berger's car and once she sees how charismatic I am, it won't matter what I drive."

The self-satisfied smirk I'd often noticed on Berger appeared on Kip's face.

In some ways Kip and Berger were like two sides of the same coin.

"You one-hundred-percent sure Berger's with his buddies at the Bon Jovi concert in Chicago?"

"Totally. They're spending the night. Before he left, he parked his car in front of Charla Sue's duplex so she can't miss it. Did you know she was Miss Prom Queen 1978 when Berger was a senior, and that he had the hots for her?" A mischievous grin spanned the width of his face. "Mom eats it up when Berger tells her he comes home for her cooking. But he's really trolling for a date with Charla Sue. What he doesn't know is she received an engagement ring from Eddie Morris two weeks ago. Not even this totally rad vehicle will help him now." He caressed the side of the car. "It would be a waste if one of us didn't use it to score a date. You in?"

"Sure." My answer was fueled more by my desire to be seen riding in a dream car than common sense, but when would I ever get another chance like this?

Kip opened the door and sank into the plush, chevron-patterned seat cover. I threw my doubts and my backpack in the trunk and slid into the passenger seat. With closed eyes, I breathed in the heady aroma of off-gassing. Ah, that new car scent. Nothing beats it.

"Look at this," Kip said, leaning over to open the glove box. "It's even got a mini-bar with magnetized shot glasses. How cool is that? Too bad there's no booze in it."

I disagreed, although I kept that to myself.

Our joy ride was a rocky road. The car shot forward as fast as a racehorse out of the gate when Kip put his foot on the accelerator, causing him to slam on the brakes. Again and again.

"Hey," I yelled, clutching the dashboard to keep my head from hitting the windshield and bursting open like a pinata. "Take it easy."

"Eat my shorts," Kip said through gritted teeth.

He finally gained control. The car didn't exactly purr like a kitten, but it was no longer a bucking bronco. Kip put the top down and a Phil Collins cassette in the player, the stars shone bright in the cloudless summer sky, and we didn't have a care in the world.

By the end of the evening, the car had worked its magic. Kip had impressed Paula, copped a feel or two in the back seat, and landed a Saturday night date. I made out, too. I got to drive the dream car.

After we returned Paula to her friends, Kip took over the wheel. We cruised around, enjoying the envious looks we received. Then Kip turned onto a street known as Drag Racing Central.

This was bad news. "What are you doing?"

"Relax. It doesn't hurt to hang out. See what's going on."

I'd seen that look on Kip's face before. The last time, it had cost me two weeks detention after school.

Within minutes a black Corvette challenged us to a race. He revved his engine. Kip revved back, his eyes bright as he nodded his acceptance.

"Have you lost your mind? If Berger finds out—"

"But he won't. Now sit back and enjoy. I heard Berger tell one of his pals that this baby can do 150 MPH without throwing a rod."

We were in the right-hand lane, the cars side by side. Kip pulled ahead keeping the Corvette from passing us. It slowed down and swerved into our lane to avoid hitting a car at the same time Kip braked hard to avoid hitting a dog. The sound of metal on fiberglass was sickening. The world seemed to stop temporarily, then sped up and spit us out into real time. I pinched myself. Hard. I was okay.

The Corvette sped off, its driver waving his fist in the air.

"Damn," Kip cried. "That jerk didn't even stop to see if we were hurt. You okay?"

My teeth had clattered together so hard I hoped I hadn't cracked a tooth. "Yes, Kip. Never better."

My sarcasm didn't register with him. He pulled into the nearby movie theater parking lot and we got out.

He leaned in close to inspect the damage. "I'm so screwed," he said, his face as pale as the crescent moon. One taillight was broken, and the bumper hung at a precarious angle. A dent cratered the rear end. "Damn! Why couldn't he have hit us on the left side? We could have parked the car back in front of Charla Sue's and let Berger think someone sideswiped it."

After exclaiming "Oh my God" about a thousand times, he asked the question I was dreading: "What'll we do now?"

Kip's been my best bud ever since I moved next door ten years ago, but no way was I taking any responsibility for this mess. After all, I'd tried to talk him out of it. I backed away. "Now, wait a minute—"

Kip scratched his head, then came up with a plan after his usual two seconds of thought. "The way I see it, we got two choices—one, leave the car in a bad area of town, or two, dump it in Geist Reservoir. Either way, Berger will assume it's been stolen and call the cops. If the car's been stripped, they'll blame the gangs. If we dump it in the reservoir, it might never be found."

He didn't give me the opportunity to weigh in. "I like the second option. We drive it to a desolate spot along the reservoir and push it in. Let's go."

What? No way was I going to muck around and potentially get caught destroying stolen property. This night had gone from memorable to maniacal. "Hey, Dude, we need to think this through. It's been raining for the past three days. What if the car gets stuck in mud and we can't push it in? Even if we do push it in and it sinks to the bottom of Geist, how would we get home? The reservoir's a good twenty miles away."

"Okay, then, we'll dump the car somewhere off W. 38th Street. That's gang territory and a bus route runs along there."

Gang territory. We'd be heading straight into a danger zone. At one in the morning. How could he spout off something like that so matter-of-factly without turning green and puking his pizza all over the side of the car? "Wouldn't it be better to tell Berger and take it like a man? He has the connections to get his car fixed for next to nothing. If he discovers you dumped the car—and he will—he'll be so frosted." I held my breath, hoping sanity would prevail.

"There won't be anything to find. The gangs will strip the car to its bare bones. Don't you watch the *News at 6?*"

"But a shitload of people *have* seen us in this car. After all, that was the idea—"

"Berger will report it stolen. Cars get stolen all the time and the police don't follow through on it. They're too busy tracking down murderers. Did you know murders are up twenty-five percent in the city over last year? Berger will collect the insurance money and get another car. Problem solved."

Kip hopped in the car, and not knowing any better option, I followed. If I survived this adventure, I'd have to face the consequences of missing curfew. As Mom says, "My roof, my rules." I was so looking forward to the freedom of living in a college dorm.

We didn't make it to 38th Street.

When Kip revved the engine, two hopped-up cars pulled up on either side of us—one emblazoned with a devil motif, the other with skulls and crossbones. The drivers made Mr. T look puny. One sported dreadlocks and the other, a mullet. Both wore leather jackets boasting more studs than the couch in the teacher's lounge. Definitely not our A&W/Pizza Hut crowd.

"They're going to box us in," I yelled at Kip. "Accelerate now. Get us out of here."

The devil driver looked at me and smiled and my insides felt as if they were tied in knots.

Kip floored it. The car roared to life and lived up to its promise. The parking lot flashed by so fast I was speechless. It felt as though we were flying. I peeked out the window to make sure we were still tethered to the Earth as Kip zoomed ahead of our two assailants.

I breathed easier until a third car pulled out in front of us. Kip swerved, but still sideswiped the car, then we spun around and slowed to a crawl. The driver, with his stringy, black hair and black-and-white painted face, looked like something out of a horror movie or a rock band. He motioned for us to roll down our windows.

I wished I'd never laid eyes on this dream car, no matter how choice it was.

"You punks think you're hot shit speeding around in Daddy's car. Who's gonna pay to fix my car—"

"Hey, Dude, you deliberately got in my path," Kip yelled, nostrils flared and fist raised. "You should watch where you're going. We're not paying for a thing."

I didn't like where this was going and rolled up my window. Just in time.

"Kip, get out of here. That's not a squirt-gun ghoul guy's aiming at us."

A bullet thudded against the side window, and I almost pissed myself. Kip stepped on it as another round of bullets hit us during our retreat.

When we reached our neighborhood, I breathed easier.

"Will you look at that?" Kip asked. "There must be ten chips in the windows, and not one came through. This car is bullet-proof. Must be polycarbonate. Wicked."

Kip's great, but sometimes I swear his brains came straight out of a Cracker Jack box.

"So, Einstein? You got another plan on how to dump the car? Cause I can tell you right now, I'm not going back there."

Kip shrugged. "Can I keep it in your shed while I figure out what to tell Berger?"

Was he asking me to aid and abet? Would this put me over the line for accessory to a crime, or had I already arrived there four hours ago? I wished I'd paid better attention to those *Hill Street Blues* shows. I decided not to think about the consequences and say what any best friend would. "Sure."

I viewed our situation logically. We didn't mean any harm. We'd have to cough up some dough to fix Berger's car, but he should get a hefty discount from the guys where he worked. Everything would be fine. No reason to panic. After all, it was only a car.

* * *

My timing was perfect. I arrived at Kip's house the next morning right as Berger's buds dropped him off. I suppose it would have been too much to ask that Berger wouldn't notice his car was missing.

He and Kip were on the front porch. Berger clenched and unclenched his fists, then screamed. "If I catch the SOB who stole that car, I'll kill him." Then he did a one-hundred-eighty-degree turn and faced Kip. "Did you have something to do with this?"

"Me? No, not exactly."

I could see Kip was going to try to squirrel his way out of this one with some outrageous story. Maybe aliens from space—the *Alien*, not the *ET* variety—stole it. I headed him off. "It's in my shed."

"Your shed? What's it doing there?"

Kip fidgeted but came clean. "We took it out for a spin last night, and we had a bit of a mishap."

"A mishap? What kind of a mishap?" Berger's voice raised an octave with every word.

"Um, someone rear-ended us." Kip took a few steps back while Berger digested the info.

"You took the car without my permission? You had an accident? How much damage?"

"Nothing the guys where you work can't fix." He handed Berger the key fob.

"Let's go," Berger said as he herded us out the door and toward the shed.

Berger took one look at the car and the verbal abuse began again. "Bullet holes? You didn't mention any damn bullet holes. How the heck did that happen? On second thought, I don't want to know." He backed away and shook his head. "I can't drive the car back on the lot looking like that. They'll have my balls for ping pong practice."

"It's your car, Berger," Kip said. "Why should they care? Just tell them you got rear-ended by a get-away car being chased by the police. Shooting broke out and you were caught in the middle." His eyes shone and he grinned for the first time that day. "You could even say you and the car were instrumental in catching the criminals."

Berger wasn't buying it. "You don't understand. That's Claymore's million-dollar experimental car. With a little help from Hunter—you met him when you toured the plant, remember?—I kind of borrowed the prototype to show off to Charla Sue and the guys. If I don't take it back in one piece Monday morning, my ass is on the line. And it's your fault." Berger managed to spit that out between curse words, his face as red as the car.

I didn't dare laugh, though. Kip had temporarily gone mute, so I felt obligated to step in. I figured I couldn't make any more of a mess of it than we already had. "Berger, we'll chip in to get it repaired. I bet we could get Tony at the garage to work on it over the weekend."

"Forget it, kid. Even if you had the money, it wouldn't do any good. It's totally new technology. No one outside of Claymore's has the parts to fix it."

"Berger, how'd you get a car like that out of the plant and off the lot?" Kip asked. "Didn't you tell me and Mom the place is more secure than Fort Knox? No way Hunter would let you take it for the weekend."

"He would if you have a video of him in the breakroom doin' the nasty with the boss's eighteen-year-old daughter." Berger looped his thumbs in his belt loops, a smug look on his face. "Clever, huh?"

I wasn't sure how to respond to that, so I didn't. What I heard was that besides being a thief, Berger was a blackmailer. He had some nerve talking to us like we were criminals. A wave of relief passed over me. It was the first time my shoulders hadn't touched my ears since the accident.

Kip took Berger's confession a completely different way. "Can we see the video?" he asked.

Berger ignored him, then relayed the full story. "Hunter disabled the alarms and gave me the key fob. I drove it out of the lot to the guard station at five on Friday and told the guard I was test driving the car. There were so many cars behind me, workers all raring to begin their weekend, the guard wasn't about to check my story. Do you know what the din of fifty cars honking their horns at the same time sounds like? It's not pretty."

Then reality hit him like a punch in the gut. His shoulders sagged as he rocked back and forth on his heels muttering. About a hundred Our Fathers and that many Hail Marys would have been about right.

I realized I'd left my backpack in the car and when Berger finished bewailing his fate, I asked him to open the trunk. As I grabbed my backpack, I noticed something shiny and hard had spilled out of the damaged side pocket. A *lot* of shiny somethings. They looked suspiciously like diamonds.

"Um, Berger, what are a bunch of diamonds doing in your car?"

"What?"

"Let me see," Kip said pushing forward. He grabbed one of them, then scooped up the others in his hands and pocketed them. "This is epic. There must be at least a million-bucks worth here. We're rich!"

"No, Kip," I said. "We're in deep doo-doo. We need to call the police."

* * *

We walked back to Kip's house in silence. Berger, who dripped sweat and had acquired a twitch I hadn't noticed before, made the call. He'd just hung up when someone banged on the front door loud enough to make Mrs. Berrettini's Hummel figurines dance on the shelves.

"That was fast," Kip said. "Guess the cops were in the neighborhood." He went to the window and peeked out. "It's Hunter. With two dudes who look like Arnold Schwarzenegger from *The Terminator*. Hunter looks as if he's been in a wrestling match and lost. Should I let them in?"

That proved to be a moot question. The door shuddered one more time and all three of them barged in, leaving the front door dangling on broken hinges.

"Hey, you broke our door," Kip said.

I kicked him in the shin to encourage him to shut up. He didn't get the hint.

"Mom just bought that door. She's gonna' be so mad."

"Not as mad as when she sees what I'm going to do to you if you don't shut up," said the smaller of the two Arnolds, pushing Kip toward the dining room. "Everybody sit."

Berger finally came out of his stupor. "Hunter, what the hell? What's this all about? Who are these people?"

The bigger Arnold didn't give Hunter a chance to respond. "I'll tell you what this is all about. You've got something of mine. Thirty-six things of mine." He flexed his full-sleeve tattoo "I want them back."

I gulped and murmured a few Hail Marys myself. And I'm not Catholic.

Arnold the Large glared at Berger. "Now where's that car?"

"In the shed next door," Berger managed to say.

"Give me the key fob."

Burger pulled it out of his pocket and placed it on the table.

The bigger goon smiled. "Glad you're cooperating like your good buddy, Hunter. He saved his bacon by showing us where you'd be. Now, everyone put your hands behind your chair. We're going to make sure you sit tight."

He grabbed some rope from a duffel bag he'd brought with him and tied us up. How the heck had a simple joy ride come to this?

"Arrivederci, suckers."

He pulled a couple hundred-dollar bills from his duffel bag and threw them on the table as they left. "This ought to cover the door."

"Hunter, as soon as I'm loose, I'm going to punch you from here to Cincinnati," Berger said.

"Hey, it's not my fault," Hunter said. "You're the one who blackmailed me into giving you the car. I had no idea our boss is part of a diamond smuggling operation. When the goons informed Raider the car was missing, he had them pay me a visit. I overheard him say that when we send our cars to Canada for finishing touches, someone in the Canadian plant hides the diamonds in the cars.

"Smart trick," Kip said. "I think I saw that once on *Miami Vice*."

"And did you remember that those diamonds aren't in the car?" I asked. "When they find out they're missing, it's not just your Mom's new door that's going to take a beating."

Hunter looked puzzled.

"We found the diamonds by accident," I said. "Literally. Kip pocketed them."

A car door slammed nearby. I knew it was wishful thinking, but I hoped the two goons were taking off in the car. That didn't happen, but my second wish came true. Like on *Hill Street Blues*, the uniformed policemen called out who they were, then rushed through the broken door, guns drawn.

Berger burst out. "We're okay. The guys you want are at the shed next door, but they'll be back any minute now."

"Okay. We'll be ready for them," the female cop said. "Nelson, call for reinforcements."

Kip piped up. "They'll see your car out front."

"Unmarked. Any other entry?"

"In the kitchen," Burger said, nodding toward the back of the house.

Both policemen positioned themselves in the hallway, off the dining room. We didn't have long to wait. The goons burst through what was left of the front door and stood in front of us, glaring.

"Where's the diamonds?" the bigger one asked. He drew a knife and held it in the air so we could all see it, then he stepped in front of me. "Tell me, or I'll slit his throat." He glanced at Kip. "Bet your mom won't like cleaning his blood off her dining room rug. If I cut him just right, his blood will spray all over the curtains, too."

At that point, I passed out. When I came to, Kip's hands were untied, and he was handing over the diamonds.

"You're not going to get away with this," Berger said, all macho man with the police nearby.

The guy chuckled. "We'll be long gone before anyone finds you. And what are you going to say? After all, you stole the car. We didn't."

I wondered why the cops hadn't done anything yet. They must need the goons to further incriminate themselves. I mustered up some courage to make up for passing out earlier. "You guys got a good operation going—planting diamonds in cars at the Canada plant, then retrieving them when they reach the States."

"It was a great gig, but this is the last job we're pulling at Claymore's. We'll be out of the country in a few hours."

The other thug's eyes brightened. "Can we off them? Tie up all loose ends?" He pulled his knife from his waistband and smiled when he saw our fear.

His eagerness to kill made me sick. What were those cops waiting for? Happy hour?

"Nah. Not necessary. These guys aren't going to go to the cops. They're in a shitload of trouble already. I'd like to hear how they explain the damage to Claymore's baby, though." They laughed as they turned to leave.

Both cops appeared, in what looked like a synchronized dance routine. "Hands up where we can see them," the female cop said to the thugs. "Now lie face-down on the floor with your arms behind your back." She cuffed them in thirty seconds flat. "Nelson, keep them from talking to each other until the cars come to take them back to the station. I'm going to talk to these young men and see if I can get a handle on what happened here." She inspected the gym bag and found several guns, the diamonds, and a bundle of cash. Finally, she cut the ropes that bound us.

At first, she focused on Hunter and Berger. "Who, at your plant, was working with these guys?"

"That would be our boss, Mr. Raider." Hunter said. "He's the one who gave me up to those two guys when they discovered the car was missing."

"You didn't know anything about their smuggling operation?"

"Hell, no. You think I would have let Berger have the car if I'd known?"

"Hey, you would have done anything to keep Raider from seeing that video of you and his daughter going at it," Berger said.

"Ah, I take it there was some blackmail involved in obtaining the car?"

Hunter nodded. Berger pursed his lips and shut up.

"You know who's involved on the Canadian side?" she asked Hunter.

He shook his head. "Sorry."

She turned toward me and Kip. "How did you two get involved?"

Kip replied. "We took the car for a ride when Berger was at a concert last night. Someone pulled a gun on us, forced us out of the car, and took off in it."

"I see," the cop said. "Lucky for you, they were kind enough to drop the car back and put it in your buddy's shed the next morning." She turned toward me. "Does that sound about right?"

I could almost see my Purdue scholarship flying out the window. I ended up spilling my guts and told her the entire story. "Ma'am," I asked, "how much trouble are we in?"

"Let's see," she said as she turned toward Berger. "You're the one who stole the car from Claymore's, right?"

"I didn't steal it. I borrowed it for a couple days to impress everyone back home. Especially Charla Sue."

She turned toward Kip and me. "Did you two know it was 'borrowed'?"

We both shook our heads.

"We thought it was Berger's car, ma'am," Kip said.

"Why did you take a joy ride in your brother's car without telling him?"

Kip hung his head. "I knew he wouldn't let me within ten feet of it, and I wanted Paula to see me driving it and go out with me."

I answered before she could set her sights on me. "I wanted a chance to drive a really cool car."

I swear the cop almost smiled, although she laid into us and gave us a lecture as good as the ones Principal Fisher used to give us.

She nodded toward the bills on the table. "Did the perps give this to you?"

We nodded.

She pulled on a pair of gloves, scooped them up, and put them in an evidence bag.

"Hey, that's ours," Kip said, trying to grab them.

"Not unless you want to be arrested for passing counterfeit bills," she said. "From what we overheard, there's a lot we could charge the four of you with—theft, blackmail, attempting to dispose of stolen property, lying to the police. You want to go for spreading counterfeit money, too?

We shook our heads as ferociously as a dog after a swim in the lake.

"Good. Here's what we're going to do. We've been tracking these two crooks for months. Now we have them, thanks to you, in the nick of time. Under the circumstances we'll recommend that Claymore's, who we've been working with, drop any charges they may consider against you. It's not good PR for the company to be associated with diamond smugglers or to appear vulnerable to criminals. But that's a recommendation only. They may decide to move forward with it."

"Now, you two," she said, giving Kip and me the once over. "I hope you've learned your lesson."

"Yes, ma'am," Kip said. "It never pays to try and impress the girls."

# The Future's So Bright,
## I Gotta Wear Shades
### Joseph S. Walker

The fraternity Seth Bell belonged to wasn't actually, *officially*, named Tappa Kegga Brew, but that's what everybody on campus called it, including the brothers, who prided themselves on having wilder parties, hotter girlfriends, and more humiliating hazing than anyone else in the school's Greek system. They also had lower grades, though they tended not to talk as much about that. The eternal TKB revelry, which erupted into full-blown hedonistic excess every weekend, sometimes died down to a few brothers on the front lawn playing beer pong before morning classes, but it didn't stop, certainly not for any such trifling concern as studying.

Which made it somewhat confounding that Seth and almost two dozen of his brothers were enrolled in what was notoriously one of the most difficult courses the college had to offer: Physics 376, Subatomic Mechanics and Nuclear Theory. Three times a week, the TKB crew dutifully trooped into the auditorium at Lincoln Hall and took their seats. They were even on time, since attendance was mandatory, and zealously recorded by half a dozen teaching assistants.

Invariably, it was the professor, Dr. Raymond Motley, who was late.

At five or ten past the hour he stumbled through the door at the front of the classroom, his salt-and-pepper hair sticking out wildly in every direction, his clothing mismatched and garish, his eyes concealed behind heavy black sunglasses. He stood for a moment, seemingly startled to discover banks of students with pens poised expectedly over notebooks, then shuffled to the overhead projector next to the podium at the center of the auditorium stage. He pulled a transparent sheet, apparently chosen at random, from his ancient leather messenger bag, put it on the projector, and turned on the lamp, throwing an incomprehensible diagram or a series of insanely complicated mathematical equations on the screen. It was unclear how he could even see the image through his shades. He began talking without context or preamble, occasionally gesturing vaguely at the screen, his voice audible only to the first few rows of students until a teaching assistant hurried on stage and pressed a microphone into his hands. Once Motley worked out the function of this curious object—which generally took him a few minutes—he resumed, exactly where he had left off. He did not accept questions. At precisely ten to the hour he stopped talking, even if he was in the middle of a sentence, took his page from the projector, and walked out, often pursued by the same assistant, now trying to reclaim the mike.

Seth never had the faintest idea what Motley was talking about. Neither did any of the other TKB brothers. They didn't care, because the course grade was based purely on attendance and the course final. Dr. Raymond Motley had, in the estimation of TKB, one outstanding quality as a teacher: he had given exactly the same final exam to every class for the last ten years. All they had to do was memorize the answer key, zealously preserved in the frat's files, and they would have nice, shiny As to counterbalance some of their more egregious academic sins.

It was a fine system, until it wasn't.

* * *

Seth was in the TKB basement, setting up a Ms. Pac-Man game cabinet the brothers had recently liberated from the arcade in the student union. The frat's final group of 1986 pledges would play a tournament on the machine during the coming weekend's initiation. They hadn't yet been told that they'd be playing by standing on a stool, dropping trou, and inserting the joystick between their butt cheeks, nor that the losing pledge would be painted yellow and deposited in the middle of the quad wearing only a pink hair ribbon.

Seth was trying to decide whether to coat the joystick in hot sauce or sprinkle it with itching powder when Mitch Oswalt, TKB's president, poked his head in. "You are summoned to ascend, Brother Bell," he said. "Emergency council assembly."

"Don't tell me. A pledge complained to the student paper again."

"Worse. Let's go."

Seth followed Mitch upstairs to the dining room, where the members of TKB's executive council held conclaves around the big table. Mitch gestured Seth to an empty seat and took his own place at the head. A pledge standing in the corner of the room, wearing an elaborate ball gown, stepped forward, put a crown on Mitch's head, and backed away, eyes lowered.

"Brothers," Mitch said. "It's my sorrowful duty to inform you that TKB is faced with an existential catastrophe which has the potential to shake our beloved institution of brotherly community and mutual support to its very foundations."

The immediate response to this was confused silence. Several of the brothers looked uncertainly at each other.

"We got a big problem," Bobby Bennenzo translated. BB always sat at Mitch's right hand, primarily to issue such clarifications.

"We are, if the narrative which has reached our ears is reported aright, bedeviled by the insidious machinations of an overzealous commitment to educational reform, a shocking assault by a hidebound administrative authority on the bedrock principles of academic autonomy," Mitch said solemnly.

"We heard something real scary," BB said.

"Summon brother Payton, that the ghastly tale may be shared, its ramifications contemplated."

"Hey, skidmark," BB said to the ballgowned pledge. "Send Tank in, then get lost."

Enos Payton, universally known as Tank, was far and away the biggest member of TKB, renowned for his ability to carry three full beer kegs up a flight of stairs. He sat gingerly in the chair at the foot of the table. Tank had long ago learned that he had to be delicate with furniture. Whether he had learned anything since was a matter of lively debate.

"Brother Payton," Mitch said. "Unfold the grim news, that all may hear and know of the peril overhanging them."

"Tell them what you told us," BB echoed.

Tank shifted his weight, causing the chair to groan ominously. "You guys know my sister Alice."

General nods. Some of the assembled knew Alice considerably better than they'd care for Tank to be aware of.

"She's got a part-time gig doing secretary stuff in the physics department," Tank went on. "She told me that yesterday Doc Motley got called in by the head of the department, and they left the door kinda cracked, so she could hear what they were talking about. The guy was yelling at Motley about giving the same test every year cause it screws up all the records. He said Motley has to make up a whole new test, starting this semester."

A wave of consternation rippled around the table. Seth felt sick to his stomach. Several brothers began talking at once, while others sat frozen, heads in their hands.

Once upon a time, TKB owned a gavel. When it was lost, some of the brothers visited an adult novelties store out on the interstate, bought the two largest toys they could find, and taped them together into a T shape. Mitch used it now, dildoing the table fiercely as BB called for order.

"Relay the sequel, Brother Payton."

"Tell us the rest, Tank."

"Motley told his boss he has a new test ready to go on his home computer. All original questions. Guaranteed to flunk half the class."

"Gentlemen," Mitch said. "Brethren. The future of TKB hangs in the balance."

"If we all fail that class, the whole frat gets closed down," BB said.

"Let's kill him," Troy Zuniga said.

Seth worried about Troy sometimes.

"For the nonce we need not resort to such desperate measures," Mitch said. "We have already formulated a stratagem which should achieve our ends without quite so extreme a violation of statutory regulations."

"We've got a plan," BB said. "It's risky, but we think we've got the man to pull it off." He looked directly at Seth. "Think you're up for it, Bell?"

"Me?" Everybody at the table was suddenly looking at Seth. "What the hell can I do?"

"Employ your idiosyncratic skills and qualifications to penetrate Motley's domicile and retrieve the figurative grail," Mitch said.

"Break into Motley's house and make a copy of the new test," BB added.

"You know, I don't think we've really explored all the dimensions of the killing him idea," Seth said. "Let's kick that around for a while."

Zuniga leaned forward, eyes bright. "I've got a machete. Give me a couple of days and I can build a flamethrower."

"Desist," Mitch said. "We have every faith that Brother Bell will carry out this mission successfully."

"Based on what? Why me?"

"Two things," BB said. "First, you're the only one in the frat with a computer. Most of us wouldn't know how to turn the damn thing on, let alone find the test."

Seth tried to think of an objection to that, and came up empty. "What's the second thing?"

"Your ocular nocturnal predilections," Mitch said.

"My whatsit?"

"We figure you're the sneakiest on account of how you spend some of your evenings," BB said.

"Oh," Seth said. "That."

"That," BB confirmed.

Plenty of the brothers indulged in what Mitch might have termed trifling divergences from the strict confines of conventional legality.

Brother Birch shoplifted. Brother Timons always had spray paint with him and loved defacing traffic signs. BB himself had a thing for hot-wiring cars to make beer runs. And Seth? Seth was a peeping tom. Many nights, dressed head to toe in black, he was out in the neighborhoods around campus, seeing how close he could get to lighted windows. The ultimate thrill, of course, was catching people in the midst of carnal pleasures, but even watching a family have dinner around the TV was enough to kick his endorphins into overdrive. It was like having x-ray vision, gazing into the private little worlds people thought they had all to themselves.

"There's a big difference between peeking in a window and breaking into a house," he said.

"Well, we can hardly send Tank," BB said. "You got a better idea?" He held up a hand in Zuniga's direction without looking at him. "And I don't mean the machete. Has anybody at all got something else to suggest?"

There was a long moment of silence, broken only by Zuniga's quiet mumbling that nobody ever wanted to go with the machete.

"We could, of course, apply ourselves and endeavor to actually pass the examination on our own merits," Mitch finally said. That was one of the things that made him a good leader. He always knew when the tension needed to be broken with a joke.

"Let's say I do this insane thing," Seth said when the laughter died down. "What's in it for me? I'm risking actual jail time here."

"A job at my father's advertising firm after you graduate," BB said promptly. "Guaranteed fifty thousand a year to start."

"You can make that happen?"

"*If* you succeed."

Seth wavered, weighing prison against what he could buy with fifty thousand dollars. He'd never have to bum a couple bucks for a six-pack again, he knew that much. "Can I have a few days to think about it?"

"No," Mitch said.

"The physics faculty is having a banquet tonight for some kind of visiting science guy," BB said. "Motley will be there. It's the only time we know of to be sure he won't be home." He looked at his watch. "You should go get into whatever you want to wear. Motley's probably on his way to campus now."

Seth didn't remember actually agreeing to this plan, but looking around the table, he saw nobody prepared to debate the point any longer. He stood, and the brothers on either side of him clapped him on the back. "You can do it, man," somebody said. "We're all behind you."

Probably what the gladiators heard on their way to meet the lions. *Screw it*, Seth thought. *Look on the bright side.*

"You assholes are going to owe me *big*," he said.

* * *

Dr. Motley lived alone in a two-story blue Victorian a few blocks south of campus, a neighborhood of winding, narrow streets and expansive yards. Most of the nearby houses had been broken up into student apartments, but Motley was the sole occupant of his.

Seth approached through the backyard, thankful for early dusk and the big, mature trees on the boundary lines between most of the lots. The two shots he'd done, before leaving the frat, were not bolstering his courage as he had hoped. His heartbeat thudded in his ears. Probably should have smoked a joint instead.

The house loomed up in front of him, a menacing shape with no light in any window. He almost turned back, but then he thought about sitting down to a Motley test completely unprepared. The house immediately got considerably less intimidating.

It took him five minutes to find a basement window at the back of the house that sat imperfectly in its frame. He could slip his pocketknife into the resulting gap to turn the latch and pull the window open. He slid through feet first and froze as soon as he hit the floor, listening for any indication that he wasn't alone in the building. The silence was absolute. After a long minute he slipped a small flashlight from his pocket. The room he was in held only a few dusty boxes and an ancient metal bedframe draped in cobwebs. He slipped through the door and found himself at the bottom of a flight of stairs.

His blood was buzzing now, fear giving way to a heightened version of his familiar excitement. This was a thrill beyond peeping. He was actually inside another person's life, roaming freely and unknown, everything open to him. There were a thousand people he could think of whose homes would have interested him more than Motley's, but for the moment that hardly seemed to matter. Seth Bell felt the heavenly blessing of understanding himself in a new, deeper way. This would not, he already knew, be the last time he found a way into an empty home.

He pushed the thought to the side. He couldn't get distracted. There was a job to do here.

Upstairs, he killed the flashlight and navigated through the house by the dim glow from the streetlamps outside. The ground floor held a kitchen with a sink full of unwashed dishes, a dining room that felt long neglected, a living room dominated by a fully stocked bar (he resisted the temptation to give his earlier drinks some company), and a library lined with floor-to-ceiling bookshelves. No computer. He made his way to the second floor, holding his breath, and reached a landing with four doors standing open. The first one he looked into was obviously Motley's bedroom, with a king-sized poster bed at the center. Next was a bathroom, then a guest room, the unmade bed stacked high with packages and miscellaneous household junk. Finally, he hit paydirt: an office. He sighed in relief at the sight of the boxy computer in the middle of the desk.

He sat in Motley's swivel chair, which wobbled and creaked alarmingly, and examined the computer. It was the same model as the one his parents had sent him to college with, having been persuaded by an enthusiastic salesman at Sears that it would practically do Seth's homework for him. Seth used it to play video games and print flyers for frat events. He had freshmen to do his homework for him.

He turned the machine on and listened to its chittering booting-up noises as he flipped through the little box of five-inch floppy disks that sat next to it. Thankfully, the disorder visible in much of the house did not extend to Motley's actual work. Each disk had a carefully applied label, though Seth had to hold his flashlight close and squint to make anything of the professor's sprawling, spidery handwriting. Most had the word "Research" or "Data," followed by a number. Probably Motley had a list somewhere of what was on each disk. Some of the labels made little sense to Seth—*Recruits?, Timbuk, Apartment*—but finally he hit one simply marked "376." The course number for TKB's class.

He inserted the disk and scanned the list of files. Most were named *Lecture*, followed by a number, but there was also *Roster, Attendance, Assistants,* and, he saw with a wave of giddy relief, *New Test* and *New Test Answers.*

Too soon to celebrate. He still had to actually escape with the prize. A dot matrix printer squatted next to the computer, so at least he wouldn't have to copy everything out by hand. He turned it on and made sure that the ribbon of perforated pages was fed into it correctly. For a terrifying moment after he hit the *print* command, nothing happened. Then the lights on the printer blinked, it made a noise like a troll clearing its throat, and the printhead began moving across the page. The chittering clatter it made, and the thunk of the paper being advanced by the sprockets catching the holes on the sides, seemed, in Seth's heightened state of awareness, a little less noisy than a jet getting ready for takeoff.

*New Test* was two pages. *New Test Answers* was twenty, even longer than the answer key the frat possessed for the old test. *That's gonna be fun to memorize.* Seth paced around the room as the paper crawled through the printer a line at a time, occasionally parting the blinds a bit to peer out at the empty street. So far, everything was going smoothly.

He tried to quiet the voice in his head telling him it was going *too* smoothly.

Finally, the printing ended. Seth tore off the long stream of pages, folded them, and, mostly from force of habit, ripped the perforated strips with the sprocket holes from the sides, dropping them in Motley's overflowing trash can. He was at the top of the stairs when he realized he needed to cover his tracks. He went back into the office, restored the disk to its place in the box, and turned off the computer and printer.

It was at that moment that he heard a door open below. Seth froze, grateful he hadn't turned on any lights. There was movement on the ground floor, then a voice, too distant to catch the words but definitely male. Had Motley brought someone home? It was a matter of common faith among the brothers of TKB that the professor was utterly unacquainted with female flesh, as befit all nerds and dweebs. Maybe not, though. Maybe Seth was going to get a little show as reward for his excellent work on behalf of his brothers.

Moving slowly, easing his weight only gradually from foot to foot, Seth went back into the hallway. There was a light on the living room below. Seth moved carefully to the wall and lowered himself to his stomach. From that position, he could look through the staircase banister into the living room.

There were two men there, neither Motley. One, leaning against the wall with his hands clasped in front of him, made Tank look like a welterweight. He wore a silver tracksuit, biceps bulging against the shiny fabric, and sported a thick, long black beard. His companion, sitting on the couch, was a slim bald man wearing a black suit that looked expensive even from this distance. He looked at his watch and said something to Tracksuit, who answered briefly. They weren't speaking English, and Seth couldn't identify the harsh-sounding language. Was this maybe the visiting scientist?

Tracksuit was stoic, but Baldie radiated impatience and annoyance, tapping his foot, cracking his knuckles, looking at his watch two or three times a minute. He didn't seem to relax until, about ten minutes after they'd arrived and just as Seth was starting to think about trying to crawl out the office window, the front door opened again. The man on the couch stood, with a tight smile and a nod to the giant, who shifted his weight and stood up a little taller.

Motley came into the room. His back was to Seth, but there was no mistaking that hair.

"Dr. Motley," Baldie said. "You were told to expect me tonight. I expected to find you at home." His accent was so thick that Seth wondered if it was partly feigned. He half expected the man to ask if Motley had seen moose and squirrel.

"There was a departmental function." Motley's voice was low, sullen. "I would have been missed. I would think you would want to avoid anything that might raise inconvenient questions."

"And I would think you would want to avoid anything that might endanger our good will." Baldie waved a hand at Motley's face. "Take off those ridiculous glasses. It's the middle of the night."

Motley sat in an armchair, taking off his heavy black shades and setting them on a small table. Seth could now see part of the left side of his face. He'd never seen Motley without the glasses before.

"You shouldn't risk coming here," Motley said. "You might be seen."

Baldie held up two fingers as he resumed his place on the couch, facing the professor. "That's twice already you've told me what I should do, Raymond. Don't do it a third time, or I'll begin to think you've forgotten the terms of our arrangement. It is not you who gives directions."

"I haven't forgotten anything," Motley said. "I'm doing the best I can."

"Are you?" Baldie leaned back and crossed an ankle over a knee. "It's been two years since you gave us Mr. Benson. I'll grant you that was a coup. We understand he will soon be attached to a new Presidential committee on nuclear power. But this is not a forgiving game, Raymond. This is not a game where you can rest on your prior accomplishments. This is a game that continually asks what you have done for me lately."

Clearly, Seth realized, Baldie was not the visiting scientist. At the moment, however, this seemed less important than his growing awareness that the rug he was stretched out on was very, very dusty, and that a good deal of that dust was finding its way into his sinuses.

"It's not as easy as it used to be," Motley said. "When I started, half the kids on campus were practically hippies. It was a piece of cake to sell them on doing something to hurt the war machine. Hell, you guys might as well have been paying Nixon, the way he was driving them right into your arms. It's not like that now. They freaking *love* Reagan. They can't wait to fight the evil empire. I whisper a word in the wrong ear and I'm going to end up in a room three floors beneath FBI headquarters, and then what good am I to you?"

"But what good are you to me now?" Baldie asked. He shook his head. "Perhaps you're right. Perhaps you can no longer be of service as you once were. But in that case, Raymond, it is not merely our association that has come to an end. You know too much for us to simply leave you loose in the world."

"Wait a minute," Motley said.

Baldie's eyes went to Tracksuit, who had been standing so still for so long that Seth had almost forgotten he was there. "Victor," he said.

Three things happened at once. Victor unzipped the front of his tracksuit and reached his right hand inside, under his left arm. Motley stood, making a wordless noise, holding out his hand.

And Seth, explosively, sneezed.

For a long, frozen moment, nobody moved. Seth spent the moment imagining leaping to his feet, making a run for the office window, and having Victor catch up to him before he could get it open and dive through, which would probably break his neck anyway.

*Fuck it. Roll the dice.*

He got his feet under him and came down the stairs, smiling broadly and keeping his eyes far away from the long black handgun Victor now held in his left hand. "Sorry, doc," he said. "Guess I spoiled the surprise."

All three of the men were staring at him, Baldie with narrow eyes, Victor with a furrowed brow, and Motley with his mouth hanging open. Victor looked straight at him, widening his grin even more and willing the professor to catch up. This was complicated by the fact that Motley, now that the glasses were off, turned out to have a lazy eye, leaving Seth a little unsure as to which one he should look at.

"The surprise," Baldie said.

"Sure," Seth said. "The doc wanted to spring me on you just when you thought he didn't have anything." Reaching the bottom of the stairs, he shrugged and tried to look abashed. "I think he was a little miffed that you were doubting him. Darn allergies ruin everything."

"Victor," Baldie said evenly. "See if this young man is carrying identification. And while you are at it, let's see what's bulging out his pocket so severely."

Victor brought the gun up. He wasn't quite pointing it at Seth, but the hole at the end of the barrel still seemed big enough to drive an eighteen wheeler through. "Hands on wall," the big man said.

Seth swallowed. "Sure thing." He turned and placed his hands on the wall. He couldn't get his shoulders to relax. A hand like a slab of beef felt quickly but thoroughly along his sides and up his legs. He felt the folded test and his wallet being removed from his pockets, then sensed Victor stepping back.

"Okay," Victor said. "Move slow."

Seth turned, moving slow. Victor was watching him carefully. Some of the color seemed to be coming back into Motley's face. Baldie was looking through Seth's wallet, the printout under one arm.

"Seth Bell," Baldie said. "This is your new offering, Raymond?"

"You bet," Seth said.

"If you please. I wish to hear this from Dr. Motley himself."

"Yes," Motley said. He looked from Seth to Baldie. "Bell. Seth Bell. A very bright young man. I believe he'll be of considerable use to you."

"And this?" Baldie held up the printout.

"The doc asked me to check over the test he made up for the class this term," Seth said. "Just to be sure there weren't any mistakes."

Baldie raised his eyebrows. "Motley trusts you to check his own work?"

Seth tried to look like someone trying to look modest. "Well, he seems to think I have the knack. Isn't that right, doc?"

Motley's eyes narrowed a fraction. "Sure," he said flatly. "Never hurts to have a second pair of eyes."

Baldie nodded slowly. He gestured at the armchair Motley had been in a moment before. "Have a seat, young man."

Seth sat, noting with relief that Victor was returning his gun to its place under his arm. Motley, looking a little dazed, fell back onto the couch. Baldie sat on the coffee table in the center of the room, his knees a few inches from Seth's. He held out the wallet and test, but as Seth reached for them, he pulled them back a few inches. "Let us be explicit, Mr. Bell, about what we can expect from each other."

Seth nodded. "Absolutely."

"You will graduate with a degree in nuclear science. You will get a job with an arms manufacturer, a major research lab, or the defense department. Yes?"

Seth spread his hands and smiled, knowing there was no possibility of any of that happening. "That's the plan."

"From time to time, I will come to you with questions or instructions. This may happen several times a year. It may happen once and never happen again. Who can say? But as long as you stay in position, as long as you answer my questions, as long as you follow my instructions, things will continue to get better for you. You will have free access to a Swiss account where we will deposit one hundred thousand American dollars each year. Yes?"

*Huh. Spying pays better than advertising.* "Sounds good to me."

"Of course," Baldie said, "the very moment any of this does not happen, the very moment it becomes clear you are of no use, that is when you stop dealing with me and begin dealing, albeit very briefly, with Victor."

"Won't be an issue," Seth said. Behind Baldie, Motley's forehead was prickled with sweat. Seth barely noticed, because the overhead projector in his mind was flashing various scenarios on his inner screen concerning what would happen if he could just get out of this room. Make for the nearest international border? Barricade TKB and let Victor and Tank slug it out? Go to the FBI?

"I'm pleased to hear it," Baldie said. He leaned over to pick up the glasses Motley had put down, and settled them on Seth's face. "Your future is a very bright one, Mr. Bell." With the glasses on, Baldie was a dim silhouette, Victor and Motley not visible at all. The pictures in Seth's mind darkened as well. He had absolutely no idea what he was going to do. The distorted shape moved, and Seth felt Baldie's rough dry hand pat his cheek twice, not quite a slap. "Let us hope it is not also a very short one."

# Free Fallin'
## Josh Pachter

The girls I meet on my late-night forays to the Hidden Agenda on Ventura Boulevard generally don't have one. No, their agendas are right out in the open: they're trolling for either a producer who will put them into the legitimate movies or a sugar daddy who will rescue them from the porn industry. I don't like to brag, but my—talent, if you'll forgive that overused word—is that I can be whoever they want me to be: wealthy industrialist, bored elder statesman, lonely widower, you name it. As a result, I am almost always able to flatter them into inviting me home with them, and after a single night of bliss I am happy never to see them again. Instead, I closet myself in my modest Reseda bungalow and pass the time content with my own company until desire sends me back to the Hidden Agenda to ingratiate myself with the next one.

Annerie, however, was different. The first thing I noticed about her—even before the lush curves that magicked her simple black cocktail dress into a satyr's wet dream—was her eyes. They were a piercing cerulean blue, and they suggested ecstasies I had never known before.

Then—eyes duly noted and catalogued—my gaze dropped to her curves, and I took the empty barstool beside her and introduced myself as Lester Lyons.

"And your name, my dear?"

"Annerie," she purred, drawing out the last syllable like a promise.

"Annerie?" I repeated, pronouncing that final vowel sound as if it were a question, an invitation to present me with her family name.

But the invitation was declined. "Just Annerie," she said, and then a flash of those infinitely blue eyes took away the sting of the rejection, and she added, "for now."

I offered to buy her a drink, and that invitation she accepted. She asked Mario for a glass of pinot grigio, and I had my usual Macallan, neat, water back.

Her voice thrilled me to my very core. If she hadn't told me early on that she was Danish, her accent would have suggested Eastern Europe rather than Scandinavia. Perhaps her parents had emigrated from behind the Iron Curtain to "the happiest country in the world."

At ten, Mario's shift ended, and Tom came on to man the stick until three in the morning, when the Agenda would close. Annerie and I sipped our drinks and chatted for an eminently pleasant hour.

Around eleven, she swallowed the last of her wine and dabbed at her red lipstick with a cocktail napkin. "Well," she said.

This was the moment when I would normally dial my charm up to maximum and make her believe that my seeing her home was *her* idea…but for some reason I couldn't explain, my normal battle plan simply didn't seem right for this exceptional woman. For the first time in a very long time, I found myself at a loss for words.

She opened her purse and looked inside it and closed it, obviously stalling to give me the opportunity to make the move I strangely felt no inclination to make.

When words came out of my mouth at last, I was as astonished to hear them as she must have been.

"Would you be interested," I said, "in taking in a movie?"

One eyebrow raised inquisitively. "At this hour?"

"There's a midnight show at the Nuart," I said. "I can call us an Uber, and we'll be in plenty of time."

"A movie," she repeated, "in L.A. Imagine that."

"It's Bela Lugosi," I said. "You're not by any chance into the old black-and-white films, are you?"

"I *love* old movies," she enthused. "But please, Lester, not one of those terrible pictures he made with that ridiculous man Ed Wood, when he was old and strung out on morphine and methadone."

She pronounced it *Et Vut,* and the sound of it—combined with the mere fact that she knew who Et Vut *vas* and was familiar with the tragedy of Lugosi's final years—sent a shiver up my spine.

"No, no," I assured her. "It's the one that made him famous."

"Ah, yes, Tod Browning's take on Bram Stoker's lovely novel." She smiled dazzlingly, cocked her head as if she could hear wolves howling, and quoted, in an eerily accurate reproduction of Lugosi's voice, "Leesen to them! Cheeldren of the night. What music they make!"

Tom the bartender cruised over to us. "Another white wine for you, miss?"

She twirled the stem of her empty glass and blessed him with that smile, though I noted approvingly that she dimmed the wattage a bit when she turned it away from me. "I never drink," she said, still quoting, and then arched her perfect eyebrows and added, "*vine.*"

* * *

The movie was wonderful. I've seen it many times, and it's always wonderful. Murnau's *Nosferatu*, the original film version of the book, is charming in its amateurish special effects, and Max Schreck is truly chilling as Count Orlok, but give me Browning's 1931 production every time.

We sat there in the theater, and at that lovely moment when Lugosi says to Edward Van Sloan, "For a man who has not lived even a single lifetime, you're a wise man, Van Helsing," I felt Annerie's slender fingers creep into mine, and we held hands like two innocent children until the house lights came up.

Back out on Santa Monica Boulevard, I offered—without ulterior motive, for once—to see her home.

"Not tonight, Lester," she said. "It's too soon. Perhaps another time."

"Will there *be* another time?" I asked.

She smiled, and her eyes flashed in the light from the theater marquee. "I think so," she said. "Yes, I think there will be."

* * *

There was. There were.

We fell easily into the habit of meeting at the Hidden Agenda three or four times a week. I offered more than once to buy her dinner, but for reasons she kept to herself she insisted on meeting at nine, no sooner. I wondered if she might have a husband, children, another life she couldn't escape until the middle of the evening, but resisted the urge to pry, and Annerie kept her own counsel.

And so we met at the bar, we drank two or three drinks she allowed me to pay for, and then we Ubered to one of the city's classic movie palaces—the Nuart, the Los Feliz, the Egyptian—whichever one happened to be showing the film we most wanted to see. Our taste in cinema was remarkably in sync: some nights we shivered with another of Universal's monsters, others we laughed with Lubitsch or Sturges or Capra, still others we watched Ginger Rogers match Fred Astaire step for step, only backwards and in high heels.

We always held hands, but that was the extent of our physical interaction. The third time we met, I tried to kiss her as I handed her into an Uber at the end of the night, but she slipped a hand between her lips and mine and whispered, "Not yet, Lester. I'll tell you when it's time."

She always told the driver to pull away from the curb before announcing her destination, so I had no idea where she lived. The thought of following her never even occurred to me. That was the sort of thing the *old* Lester Lyons might have done, but that callow fellow was rapidly receding into the dim mist of the past.

By our fifth date, I was madly in love with Annerie and almost overwhelmed with desire. Not the lustful desire of my previous—what shall I call them?—*interactions* with women, but a desire that was on the one hand much stronger yet on the other hand, I blush to use this word, *purer* than anything I had ever before experienced. It's hard to nail down what exactly it was about her that obsessed me so. The best I can do is say that I finally felt, after years of one-night stands with strangers who only interested me because of what I could get from them, as if I'd met a kindred spirit.

Our early conversations over drinks at the Agenda focused in on the usual superficial data points. She loved horses, had always wanted to own one. She'd never had the opportunity to see Elvis live, but she adored his concert videos and corny film appearances. In such ways, the two of us were polar opposites. Horseback riding held no appeal for me, and my musical taste ran to the singer/songwriters: Joni Mitchell, Billy Joel, Paul Simon, even Jimmy Buffett.

After our first few meetings, though, Annerie began to open up more, to dig below the surface of her likes and dislikes. She claimed, to my surprise, to be a Christian. Not evangelical, thank goodness, but in her own way devout. Though she detested Donald Trump and his tin-hat MAGA sheep, she still believed that America was a land of opportunity, a country in need of saving from extremists but *worth* saving. And though she never did reveal her last name, she told me of her early years, of growing up an only child in an idyllic nuclear family.

In all these ways, too, we couldn't have been more different. I am an atheist, convinced that the American experiment has irretrievably failed, and I can't even *remember* my parents, who died a very long time ago.

And yet....

And yet the connection I felt between us was undeniable. Perhaps that's how true love *works*. As Michael Franks, another singer/songwriter I admire, once put it, "Love is the pain you can't refuse."

Because it *was* painful, you see, to sit beside her in the dark, our hands intertwined but our eyes and ears fixed intently on the silver screen that loomed before us, wishing the film would go on forever but knowing that all too soon those awful words "The End" would appear and we would go our separate ways with not even a kiss to bind us until the next time.

* * *

Tonight, I found myself restless after the sun went down, but it was too early to meet Annerie at the Hidden Agenda, so I went up to the Groves Overlook to stand in the shadows and watch the lights wink on across the valley. I was excited at the prospect of seeing her again, and that excitement was a sensation I had never experienced across all my years. I felt like a teenager. I wanted to write her name in the sky and draw a heart around it.

And then finally it was time, and I was gliding down over Mulholland when I felt something sting the back of my neck. Frozen waste plummeting earthward from an airplane's flushed toilet? I looked over my shoulder and was shocked to see a *bat* keeping pace with me. *Desmotus rotundus*, with an eight-inch wingspan and those beady black eyes that struck terror into the heart of anyone unfortunate enough to cross their path.

"Get away from me!" I shouted, clapping a hand to my neck to protect it from further attack.

For just a moment, the creature's black eyes flashed a stunning cerulean blue, and a familiar voice whispered, "Too late, Lester. I'm afraid you won't be keeping our date this evening."

My own wings crackled and cracked and shattered, and as I grew despite my efforts to retain my chosen form to my full human height, my fur metamorphosed into black trousers and dinner jacket.

I had somehow never thought about it before: if a vampire's bite turns a human being *into* a vampire, what does it do *to* a vampire?

Now I knew.

My heart broken by Annerie's betrayal, I flapped my arms desperately, but it was no use. I wasn't flying anymore. I was free falling, and a red mist spread before my eyes like a flame of fire. As the ground rushed up to meet me, the only thought in my mind was that, after more than five hundred years, it was time at last for me to leave this world— not for a while, but forever.

And there are, I knew, far worse things awaiting man than death.

# *Our Totally Tubular Authors*

**Linda Kay Hardie**'s varied careers ranged from radio disk jockey to adjunct college professor. That may help explain her story here, although she reluctantly admits it also could have been due to the Spanish Torrontes wine. Or maybe the cheap scotch she drinks to forget that she can't afford decent scotch.

Linda writes horror, crime, historical, and SF/fantasy stories and poetry, plus essays (often about cats but sometimes baseball). In 2022, she was honored with the Sierra Arts Foundation's Literary Arts Award for fiction in Reno, Nevada. That came only with a check. No candy.

Linda's stories appear in many anthologies, including *A Killing at the Copa, Sex & Violins,* and *The Perp Wore Pumpkin.* She's a member of Horror Writers Association, Short Mystery Fiction Society, Queer Crime Writers, Society of Children's Book Writers & Illustrators, and Cat Writers Association. Linda is an Abyssinian Rescue Ranger, volunteering in purebred cat rescue. She works as a writer, writing coach, teddy bear builder, and staff serving purebred rescue cats.

**Steve Shrott** is an award winning writer whose short stories have appeared in numerous publications including *Sherlock Holmes Mystery Magazine, Mystery Weekly,* and *Black Cat Mystery Magazine.* In Flame Tree Press' hard cover volume, Steve's story, "The House" appears alongside tales by Author Conan Doyle and Charles Dickens. His work can also be found in the Anthony-Award-winning, Bouchercon anthology, *This Time For Sure,* and in the soon-to be-released, Malice Domestic anthology, *Mystery Most Humorous.* He also wrote the introduction and has a story in the compilation, *Die Laughing.* His comedy material has been used by well-known performers of stage and screen, and he has written a book on how to create humor (*Steve Shrott's Comedy Course.*) Two of Steve's humorous mystery novels were published--*Audition for Death* and

*Dead Men Don't Get Married* and some of his jokes are in the Smithsonian Institution. For more information and news, go to www.steveshrottwriter.weebly.com

An award winning author of nineteen historical thrillers (also available from White City Press), **Marilyn Todd** is also a prolific writer of short stories, most of which are crime, but which range from commercial women's fiction to comic fantasy and all points in between. When she isn't killing people, Marilyn enjoys cooking. Which is pretty much the same thing.

**Teresa Inge** is an award-winning mystery author. Her work appears in anthologies and novellas including *First Comes Love, Then Comes Murder* and *Gag Me with a Spoon.*

She is a member of Sisters in Crime, Short Mystery Fiction Society, and Virginia Writer's Club, and she blogs regularly on Sand in our Shorts and Writers Who Kill.

Teresa grew up reading Nancy Drew mysteries. Combining her love of reading mysteries and writing professional articles led to writing crime fiction. By day, she works for a global financial firm as an admin assistant, corporate reporter, and notary administrator. When not writing, she shows her 1955 Torch Red Thunderbird at car shows.

She lives in Southeastern Virginia with her husband and mixed-shepherd Luke and can be reached at www.teresainge.com

**Michael Bracken** (www.CrimeFictionWriter.com) is the Edgar Award, and Shamus Award-nominated, Derringer-winning author of almost thirteen hundred short stories, including crime fiction published in *Alfred Hitchcock's Mystery Magazine, Ellery Queen's Mystery Magazine, The Best American Mystery Stories, The Best Mystery Stories of the Year,* and many other publications. Additionally, Bracken is the editor of *Black Cat Mystery Magazine* and editor or co-editor of thirty-two published and forthcoming anthologies, including *Janie's Got a Gun: Crime Fiction Inspired by the Music of Aerosmith,* the Anthony Award-nominated *The Eyes of Texas: Private Eyes from the*

*Panhandle to the Piney Woods*, and, with Barb Goffman, the Derringer Award-winning *Murder, Neat*. He is a recipient of the Edward D. Hoch Memorial Golden Derringer Award for lifetime achievement in short mystery fiction and, in 2024, he was inducted into the Texas Institute of Letters for his contributions to Texas literature. He lives, writes, and edits in Texas.

**John M. Floyd** is the author of more than a thousand short stories in publications like *AHMM, EQMM, Strand Magazine, The Saturday Evening Post, Best American Mystery Stories*, and *Best Mystery Stories of the Year*. A former Air Force captain and IBM systems engineer, John is also an Edgar nominee, a Shamus Award winner, a six-time Derringer Award winner, and a past recipient of the Edward D. Hoch Memorial Golden Derringer for lifetime achievement. One of his stories recently appeared in the White City Press anthology *A Killing at the Copa*.

Cows, **Lesley A. Diehl** learned growing up on a farm, have a twisted sense of humor. They chased her when she went to the field to herd them in for milking, and one ate the lovely red mittens her grandmother knitted for her. Determining that agriculture wasn't a good career choice, instead she uses her country roots and her training as a psychologist to concoct stories designed to make people laugh in the face of murder. "A good chuckle," says Lesley, "keeps us emotionally well-oiled long into our old age." She is the author of several cozy mystery series and numerous short stories. Go to her webpage to find out more: www.lesleyadiehl.com.

**Sandra Murphy** lives in St Louis and spends much of her time communing with her imaginary friends who tell her their stories. Unlike guests who eventually leave, imaginary friends stay forever with an endless number of tales to share. Sandra also writes magazine articles, edits a newsletter, and may someday hear a story that will reach book length. Sandra is the editor of the White City Press anthologies *Sex & Violins* and *Yeet Me In St. Louis*, as well as the author of the crime short story collection *From Hay to Eternity*.

**Shari Held** is an award-winning fiction author, editor, and journalist who spins tales of mystery/crime, humor, romance, and fantasy. Her short stories have been published in more than four dozen magazines and anthologies, including *The Perp Wore Pumpkin, Sex & Violins*, and *A Killing at the Copa*, all published by White City Press. She is a member of Sisters in Crime and the Short Mystery Fiction Society. When not writing, Shari cares for five spoiled cats—three indoors and two ferals—and feeds birds, possums, raccoons, the odd groundhog, deer, and anything else that shows up in her backyard—except the coyotes. She lives in the suburbs of Indianapolis, Indiana and attends movies, reads avidly, and enjoys watching tennis matches. Visit her website, www.shariheld.com, for more information about her and her stories.

**Joseph S. Walker** ( https://jswalkerauthor.com/) is the President of the Short Mystery Fiction Society and the author of more than one hundred short stories. He has been a finalist for the Edgar, Derringer, Thriller, and Shamus Awards, and is a two-time winner of the Al Blanchard Award. His work has appeared in previous White City Press anthologies including *(I Just) Died in Your Arms: Crime Fiction Inspired by One-Hit Wonders, Janie's Got a Gun: Crime Fiction Inspired by the Music of Aerosmith*, and *Sex & Violins*. In 2023 his story *Crime Scene* became the first to be selected for both *The Best American Mystery and Suspense* and *The Mysterious Bookshop Presents the Best Mystery Stories of the Year* (marking his third consecutive appearance in this volume). He lives in Indiana.

**Josh Pachter** is an author, editor, and translator. His work has been shortlisted for the Edgar, Anthony, Agatha, Lefty, Thriller, Macavity, Derringer, and EQMM Reader awards, and he was the 2020 recipient of the Short Mystery Fiction Society's Golden Derringer for Lifetime Achievement. He has contributed stories to several previous White City Press anthologies, including *(I Just) Died in Your Arms* and *Peace, Love and Crime*. For the latest news and information, go to *www.joshpachter.com*